"I'm not going to leave my son—"

"He's not your son," Mia snapped.

"Well I might have started off as the sperm donor, but we're past that now."

"I don't want or need a man in my life. That includes you."

"Then think of it this way. I won't be the man in your life, Mia. I'll be the man in Tanner's life." Logan paused, waiting for an objection. "You're aware that you could be in danger."

A burst of air left her mouth. "I'm aware of it. I'm also aware that I wouldn't be in danger if it weren't for you."

DELORES FOSSEN

NEWBORN CONSPIRACY

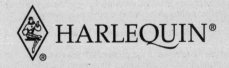

TORONTO • NEW YORK • LONDON
AMSTERDAM • PARIS • SYDNEY • HAMBURG
STOCKHOLM • ATHENS • TOKYO • MILAN • MADRID
PRAGUE • WARSAW • BUDAPEST • AUCKLAND

To Anita G. Thanks so much for answering all my
research questions.

ISBN-13: 978-0-373-88818-4
ISBN-10:   0-373-88818-X

NEWBORN CONSPIRACY

ABOUT THE AUTHOR

Imagine a family tree that includes Texas cowboys, Choctaw and Cherokee Indians, a Louisiana pirate and a Scottish rebel who battled side by side with William Wallace. With ancestors like that, it's easy to understand why Texas author and former air force captain Delores Fossen feels as if she were genetically predisposed to writing romances. Along the way to fulfilling her DNA destiny, Delores married an air force top gun who just happens to be of Viking descent. With all those romantic bases covered, she doesn't have to look too far for inspiration.

Books by Delores Fossen

Don't miss any of our special offers. Write to us at the following address for information on our newest releases.

Harlequin Reader Service
U.S.: 3010 Walden Ave., P.O. Box 1325, Buffalo, NY 14269
Canadian: P.O. Box 609, Fort Erie, Ont. L2A 5X3

CAST OF CHARACTERS

Mia Crandall—Shocked to learn that someone rigged her artificial insemination so that the father of her newborn son is dark and dangerous security specialist Logan McGrath, she has to turn to him for help when someone tries to kill her. But their immediate attraction also makes Logan a target.

Logan McGrath—When he learns he now has a son, Logan must work with Mia to protect their child and discover who's responsible for creating their child.

Tanner—Logan and Mia's six-week-old baby.

Genevieve Devereux—Logan's scheming ex-girlfriend might have orchestrated the plot to get Mia pregnant with Logan's baby.

George Devereux—Genevieve's criminal father. He would do anything to give his daughter what she wants, and what the infertile Genevieve wants is Logan's baby.

Royce Foreman—He's Genevieve's lawyer, but he also has a personal grudge against Logan. Just how far would he go to get revenge?

Donnie Bishop—The businessman might be trying to cover his illegal activity by eliminating Logan and Mia.

Collena Drake—The troubled former cop who now devotes her life to finding out what happened in the Brighton Birthing Center where Mia was artificially inseminated.

Prologue

Fall Creek, Texas

The muffled scream woke Logan McGrath.

He snapped to a sitting position in the leather recliner, turned his ear toward the sound and listened. Even through the haze of his heavy pain meds and bone-weary fatigue, he didn't have to listen long or hard to hear the raspy moans and gasps.

Someone was in a lot of pain, perhaps dying.

And that someone was on the front porch.

Because he was a man who usually dealt with worst-case scenarios, Logan automatically considered that this might be a burglar or a killer. But since he was at his brother's house in the tiny picturesque town of Fall

Creek, which wasn't exactly a hotbed of criminal activity, he had to consider another possibility: that his brother, a doctor, had a visitor, a patient who was about to die on the porch. It made sense since there wasn't a hospital in town.

Just to be safe, Logan grabbed his Sig-Sauer from the end table next to him and maneuvered himself out of the chair. Not easily. It took effort. Lots of it.

He cursed the intrusion, the throbbing pain and the unidentified SOB who'd put a .38 jacketed slug in his right leg four days ago—on Christmas day, no less.

Some Christmas present.

Logan wore only his bathrobe and boxers, and he considered a detour to the guest bedroom for a shirt and shoes. But after two steps, he changed his mind. If someone was truly dying on the porch, they'd be long dead before he could get dressed and back to him.

Another moan. Another muffled scream.

Yep, he had to hurry. Logan jammed his cane onto the hardwood floor to get better traction, and with thirteen excruciating steps, he made it to the door. He aimed his gun, and braced himself for whatever he was about to have to deal with as he glanced out a side window.

The sun was just starting to set, but there was still plenty of light for him to see the blue car parked in front of his brother's isolated country house. Logan had to look down, however, to see the driver.

She was lying on the porch. Her tan wool coat and long, loose dark-green dress were hiked up to her thighs, and she had her hands clutched on her swollen, pregnant belly.

She was writhing in pain.

Logan dropped his gun onto the pine entry table, threw open the door and maneuvered himself onto the porch. It wasn't freezing but it was close and he felt the chill slide over his bare chest and feet.

She turned her head, snared his gaze, and he saw the horrible agony in her earthy brown eyes.

"Help me," she begged. Her warm breath mixed with the frigid December air and created a misty haze around her milky pale face. "My water broke when I got out of the car and the pains are already nonstop."

So, not dying. In labor. Not the end of the world but still a huge concern.

She needed a doctor *now*.

Logan turned to go back inside to make the call to 911, but she latched on to his arm and didn't let go. For such a weak-looking little thing, she had a powerful grip. She dug in her fingernails and dragged Logan down beside her.

He banged his leg on the doorjamb and could have sworn he saw stars. Still, he pushed the godawful pain aside—after some grimacing and grunting of his own—and he tried to figure out what the heck he should do.

"Who are you?" he asked.

She clamped her teeth over her bottom lip, but he still heard the groan. "It's not the time for introductions," she grumbled. She fought to rip off her panties and then threw them aside. "Help me!"

"I've never delivered a baby before," he grumbled back, but Logan knew he was in the wrong position if he stood any chance of helping her.

Another of her muffled screams got him

moving. Plus, she drew blood with her fingernails. Somehow, he managed to get to the other end of her.

What Logan saw when he looked between her legs had him wanting to run for the phone again. Oh, mercy. The baby's head was already partially out and that meant they didn't have time for an ambulance to arrive.

"I think you're supposed to push," Logan suggested. Heaven knows why he said that. Maybe he'd heard it on TV. Or maybe this was just some crazy dream brought on by prescription pain meds. Man, he hoped that's all it was.

The woman obviously didn't doubt his advice, because she pushed. *Hard.*

Logan positioned his hands under the baby's head, and he watched. That long push strained the veins on the woman's neck, and it also eased the baby out farther. He didn't just see a head but a tiny face.

Realizing he had to do something, Logan pulled off his terry-cloth robe and laid it between her legs so that the baby wouldn't land on the cold wood. It was barely in time. As the woman pushed again, the baby's shoulders and back appeared.

"One more push should do it," Logan told her.

She made a throaty, raspy sound and bore down, shoving her feet against the porch. Seconds later, the tiny baby slid right into Logan's hands.

Wow, was his first reaction.

Followed quickly by *holy frickin' hell.*

Logan had experienced a lot of crazy and amazing things in his life, but he knew this was going to go to the top of his list.

"It's a boy," he let her know.

And that baby boy had some strength because he began to cry at the top of his newborn lungs. Obviously, he wasn't having any trouble breathing on his own and Logan was thankful for that. He wouldn't have had a clue what to do if there'd been complications.

Going purely on instinct, Logan bundled the bathrobe around the baby, especially around his head, and pulled him to his chest to keep him warm.

"A boy," she repeated. She sounded both relieved and exhausted.

The woman pushed again to expel the

afterbirth and then tried to sit up. She didn't make it on her first attempt, but she did it on her second. She reached for the baby. Logan eased him into her arms.

It was strange. He immediately felt a… loss. Probably because he was freezing and the tiny baby had been warm.

The mother looked down at her newborn and smiled. It was a moment he'd remember, all right. Her, sitting there with her fiery red hair haloing her face and shoulders, and the tiny baby snuggled and crying in Logan's own bathrobe.

"My son," she whispered.

And then she said something that nearly knocked the breath out of Logan.

"He's your nephew."

Oh, man. Oh. Man. It was obviously time for him to talk to his brother.

"I'll go inside and call an ambulance," he told her. He began the maneuvering it'd take to get him up. "By the way, we should probably do those introductions now. But you obviously already know that I'm Logan McGrath."

Because he was eye level with her when

he introduced himself, he saw her reaction. It was some big reaction, too. She sucked in her breath, and her mouth began to tremble.

"You can't be," she said, her voice trembling, too. "This is Finn McGrath's house."

"My brother isn't here," he told her. "He's on rounds at the hospital in a nearby town." In addition to confusing him, she'd also captured his attention with that comment and her reaction. "Who are you? Are you a *friend* of my brother?"

She frantically shook her head and put her index finger in the baby's mouth. He began to suck and stopped crying. "I need a doctor."

He wanted answers, but they would have to wait. "Come inside," he insisted. "It's too cold out here."

"I don't think I can get up. Please, just call an ambulance."

Well, he certainly couldn't help her get to her feet. He could barely get up himself. So, Logan tried to hurry as much as he could. With lots of pain and effort, he made it back into the living room. All thirteen steps. He dialed 911, reported the incident and requested an ambulance. He also requested that they contact his brother and have him accompany that ambulance to his house.

"Get the baby and mother inside ASAP," the emergency operator insisted. "It's dangerous for a newborn to be in the cold."

Logan agreed with her, hung up, then wondered how the heck he was going to accomplish that with his bum leg. He was more likely to fall than to be able to lift them. Still, he'd have to do it somehow.

With his cane clacking on the floor and his mind racing with possible solutions to his lack of mobility, Logan went back to the porch.

He got there just in time to see that it was empty. No mother. No newborn baby.

Just a lot of blood.

And the blue car was speeding away.

Chapter One

San Antonio, Texas
Six weeks later

Mia Crandall peered out the double glass doors of the Wilson Pediatric clinic to make sure there wasn't anyone suspicious lurking in the parking lot. There were a handful of cars, no one on the adjacent sidewalk and no one who seemed to be waiting for her to come out.

Everything was okay.

Well, everything but the niggling feeling in the pit of her stomach, but Mia had been living with that particular feeling for months now. She was beginning to wonder if it would ever go away.

She looked down at her newborn son,

Tanner, and smiled. He was still sleeping, tucked in the warm, soft covers of the baby carrier. For his six-week-old checkup, Mia had dressed him in a new blue one-piece baby outfit and a matching knit cap. Still, it was winter, so she draped another blanket over the top of the carrier so he wouldn't get cold. She retrieved her pepper-spray key-chain from her diaper bag and hurried out into the bitter weather.

It was already past five-thirty and the temperature had plunged since she'd first gone inside nearly an hour earlier. She'd had one of the last appointments of the day. Not accidental, but by design. The winter sun was already low in the sky and Mia hoped the duskiness would prevent her from being easily seen.

The wind slammed into her face, cutting her breath, but she kept up the fast pace until she made it to her car. During the past year, she'd learned to hurry, to stay out of plain sight, to go out as little as possible. It was second nature now.

She strapped Tanner's carrier into the rear-facing brackets mounted in the backseat and then slipped in behind the steering wheel. She started to turn on the engine, but the sound stopped her.

There was a sharp rap on the passenger's side window.

Mia's gaze whipped toward the sound and she saw a man staring at her. But this wasn't just any ordinary man.

Oh, God. He'd found her.

Choking back a gasp, Mia grabbed for the lock, but it was already too late. Logan McGrath pulled open the passenger's door and calmly got inside her car as if he had every right to do just that.

He was dressed all in black. Black pants, black pullover shirt and black leather coat. His hair was midnight black, as well, and slightly shorter than it'd been when she had seen him six weeks earlier. Maybe it was all that black attire that made his eyes stand out. They were glacier blue. Cold, hard. Demanding.

She remembered that he'd been hurt the night she had given birth to Tanner. He'd used a cane and could barely walk. But he didn't seem at a disadvantage now. She couldn't say the same for herself. He outsized her and no doubt had years of martial arts training. Still, she had something he didn't.

A maternal instinct to protect her son.

Mia forced herself not to panic. She thrust her hand in the diaper bag and located her cell phone. She was about to call 911 when Logan McGrath caught her wrist and took the phone from her. He also took her keys with the pepper spray and the diaper bag, shoving all the items on the floor next to him.

When he moved, his leather coat shifted, just a little. Enough for her to get a glimpse of the shoulder holster and gun tucked beneath it. But then, he probably didn't go many places without that firearm.

Mia lifted her chin and put some steel in her expression. There was no way she was going to let this man take control of the situation.

"Get out!" she ordered.

"Soon. I came to pick up my bathrobe. You took it with you when you left Fall Creek."

So, he obviously knew who she was. Not that he would likely forget delivering a baby on his brother's front porch. He was also obviously good with the sarcasm. Calm and cool under pressure.

Unlike her.

Her heart was beating so fast she thought it might leap out of her chest. Mia couldn't let him see that fear, though. For her baby's sake, she had to get this man out of her car. *Somehow.* And then she had to get far away from him so he could never find her again.

"I'll mail you the robe," she informed him. "Write down your address and then get out of my car."

The corner of his mouth lifted slightly. It didn't soften the rock-hard expression on his square jaw or high cheekbones. But that expression did soften when he glanced back at the infant seat.

Mia's heart dropped to her knees. God, this couldn't be happening. She'd been so stupid to go his brother's house that day. Now, that stupidity might cost her everything.

She couldn't physically fight him off,

though she would try if it came down to it. However, maybe she could defuse this awful situation with some lies.

"I'm grateful to you for delivering my baby," she said, hoping that it sounded sincere. Because she was sincere about that. The rest, however, was pure fabrication. "I went to your brother's house because I was driving through Fall Creek and realized I was in labor. I saw the MD sign on his mailbox and stopped."

He turned in the seat, slowly, so that he was facing her and aimed those ice-blue eyes at her. "How do you think I found you, Mia Crandall?"

She froze. Gave it some thought. And her mouth went bone dry. Because she couldn't speak, she shook her head.

Logan McGrath calmly reached over, locked the doors, retrieved her keys and started the engine. He turned on the heater and waited until the warm air blew over them before he continued.

"I had DNA tests run on the blood you left on the porch," he explained.

Of course he had.

Logan McGrath was a man who thought like a criminal. Too bad she hadn't wiped up after herself, but then she hadn't exactly had the time or energy for that chore. Mia had barely been able to get Tanner and herself to the car so she could get to the hospital in San Antonio. During that entire drive she'd been terrified that McGrath would follow her. His injury had probably prevented that from that happening, it was highly likely that he hadn't been able to drive.

"I'm sure you know that your DNA is on file because of your former job as a counselor in a state women's shelter," he continued. "Once I had your name, I found an address for you here in San Antonio. You'd moved, of course. So, I took a different approach to locate you."

And Mia thought she might know what that *approach* was. "You hacked or bribed your way into the appointments of pediatric clinics all over the city because you knew that I'd be taking my baby in for a six weeks' checkup."

He nodded. "*Hacked* is not quite the right word. I had police assistance to help me put all the pieces together." He lifted his hands, palms up in an exaggerated gesture. "And here we are."

"Not for long." Because she needed something to do, Mia clutched the steering wheel until her knuckles turned white. "Look, if you want money because you delivered my baby—"

"You know what I want, and it's not money. It's not my robe, either. I want answers."

Mia glared at him. "No. No answers. Get out of my car and out of my life."

"That's not going to happen."

He leaned closer, violating her personal space. He smelled dangerous. And very virile, which she was sorry she'd noticed.

"Let me help you with those answers," Logan continued, his Texas drawl easy but somehow dark. "I already know a lot about you, Mia Frances Crandall. Born and raised in Dallas, you've had a tough life. When you were fifteen, two drug-crazed teen burglars broke into your home, murdered your parents and left you for dead."

Mia automatically touched her fingers to

her throat, to the scar that was still there. It was faint and barely visible now. Unlike the invisible wounds beneath.

Those scars would never fade.

"I don't have time for a trip down memory lane," she grumbled. She forced back the brutal images of that night in Dallas. "I need to get home. My baby will be waking up soon and will want to nurse." Now, she leaned closer, hopefully violating his space. "Nurse, as in breast-feed. You might make your living doing shocking, violent things, but I'm guessing you'd be very uncomfortable watching me nurse Tanner."

Something went through his eyes. *"Violent things?"* He looked genuinely insulted.

Mia wanted to curse. Now, he obviously knew that she was aware of who he was. She just kept getting deeper and deeper into this hole she was digging.

"I own a private security company," he corrected.

Since there was no going back, Mia just charged forward. "You lend your services and your guns in war zones," she challenged.

"Occasionally." He lifted his shoulder. "When it's necessary to rescue people and protect American interests abroad."

Mia huffed. "That's semantics. You're an international hired gun."

"I'm the good guy." He hitched his thumb to his chest.

"That's debatable." ·

"Says who?" he fired right back at her.

Now, she put her thumb to her chest. "Me."

There was slight change in his breathing pattern. It became heavier, as if he were annoyed.

"We obviously have strong opinions about each other," he concluded. "Care to hear my opinion about you?"

"No." And Mia didn't even have to think about that.

"Tough. You're going to hear it. A little less than a year ago, right around your twenty-eighth birthday, you decided that you wanted to have a baby. There was no man in your life, no immediate prospects of marriage, so you went to Brighton Birthing Center just outside San Antonio. They have a fertility clinic there, and you made arrangements to be artificially inseminated. It was successful. You got pregnant on your first try."

He knew.

Mercy, he knew.

"How did you learn that?" she asked, swallowing hard.

"Careful investigative work over the past six weeks."

"It's not illegal to use artificial insemination to become pregnant. It's a private matter. And it's none of your business."

Even though she knew it was his business.

Hopefully, he didn't know that.

He opened his mouth, closed it, and waited a moment. During that moment, he looked even more annoyed. "I don't know why you did what you did, but obviously something started to go wrong. You got suspicious of the Brighton Birthing Center. So, days before the center was closed because of illegal activity, you made an appointment with your fertility counselor, and when the counselor left the room to get you a glass of water that you requested, you took some files from the counselor's desk drawer."

Mia hadn't thought it possible, but her heart beat even faster. "If I did or didn't do that, it's still none of your concern."

"But it's true. I managed to get my hands on some surveillance tapes. You took two files."

That was correct. Unfortunately, it'd also been a mistake. Mia had intended to take only her own file that day. She'd taken the other one accidentally because it had been tucked inside hers.

She wished to God that she'd never seen that file.

"The police have already questioned me about this," she admitted. "They agreed that I was right to have had doubts about Brighton. I gave them the files I'd taken and they let me go. End of story."

"Not even close. What made you suspicious of Brighton?"

She almost refused to answer, but maybe he knew something about this, as well. Maybe the tables would be reversed and he could provide her with some answers.

"Someone was following me," she explained. "Then once, someone actually tried to kidnap me. After that incident, I went to the police and they found a miniature tracking device taped on the undercarriage of my car. By then, there were rumors that Brighton was being investigated for illegal adoptions and lots of other criminal activity."

He shrugged. "So why take the files?"

"I thought I was just taking *my* file. I wanted to make sure there were no…irregularities. Because by then, I'd gone through the insemination and was nearly five months pregnant. I wanted to verify that they hadn't done anything that would ultimately harm my baby."

That earned her a flat look.

"And you know the other file that you took was mine," he tossed out there to her.

Because Mia didn't think it would do any good to deny it, she nodded. "I don't know how it got mixed in with mine."

"Don't you?"

Surprised with his increasingly icy accusations, she shook her head. "No. I don't."

"Did you read the file?" he demanded.

"I glanced at it, because I didn't know what it was at first. I thought it was part of my records."

He made a sound to indicate he didn't believe her. "I'll bet you did more than glance. But then, you already knew what was in it, didn't you? You're the reason that file was at Brighton."

Stunned, Mia stared at him. She hadn't expected him to say that. Nor did she know why he'd said it. "I don't know what you mean."

"Of course, you do. Five years ago, I was diagnosed with Hodgkin's lymphoma. I'm cured now, but because my treatment could have left me sterile, I decided to stockpile some semen. It was stored in Cryogen Labs, here in San Antonio. That file you took, the one tucked inside yours, was my file from Cryogen." He paused. "What I want to know is why you did it?"

Tired of the ambiguous questions, Mia threw out her hands. "Did what?"

He huffed as if he thought she were stonewalling him. But she wasn't. Mia had absolutely no idea what he was talking about.

"He's your nephew," he said, enunciating each syllable. "That's what you said right

after I told you that you'd had a son. You said that because—"

"I was delirious." Her voice was so filled with breath that it hardly had sound.

"No. You said it because you thought it was true. You thought I was my brother. Therefore, you thought my brother had a nephew. And since he's my only sibling, there's only one conclusion I can draw from that."

Logan McGrath stared at the carrier seat. "Judging from what I've uncovered, the little boy that I delivered is my own son."

Chapter Two

"My son," Logan mumbled, in case Mia Crandall hadn't heard him.

But, of course, she had heard every word. She sat there, shaking her head and looking…terrified.

That wasn't quite the reaction he'd expected. He'd thought she would at least look a little guilty.

"Why did you do it?" he asked. And this time, he would get an answer.

"Do what?" she argued.

He groaned. He was already tired of this game. "Why did you use my semen to have yourself inseminated?"

"I didn't." And there wasn't a thread of doubt in her denial. "I asked for an anonymous donor."

Figuring that it would intimidate her, he stared into her eyes, not plain brown as he thought when he first saw her on the porch. They were rich dark amber with flecks of honey gold that were nearly the same color as her loose sweater and coat. Memorable eyes.

As was the woman herself.

Despite what he thought about her—and his thoughts about her were pretty bad—Logan had to admit that Mia Crandall was damn attractive. It was in part the hair, he decided. He'd always been a sucker for a redhead and she had that in spades. Her hair was long and thick; it framed her ivory-pale aristocratic face.

However, it was also her mouth that caught his attention. Full and lush. Nothing aristocratic about that part of her anatomy. That mouth stirred something primitive and male deep inside him.

But he wouldn't let that get in the way of what he had to do.

Besides, he didn't need another redhead in his life.

"I was shocked when I saw your file,

because I'd requested someone with light-colored hair." She combed her gaze over him. His hair was incredibly dark. In fact, for some missions Logan had posed as an Italian, a Greek and even someone of Lebanese descent. No one had ever questioned that foreign pretense.

She paused and stared at him. "Mercy, do you actually believe that I arranged to make *you* my baby's biological father?"

"You bet I do."

Well, he'd believed it until a few moments ago, anyway. Now, after seeing her shocked and disgusted reaction, Logan wasn't so sure.

He hoped like the devil that her mouth and hair weren't responsible for this wavering of his beliefs. Just in case it was, Logan forced himself to remember that all the evidence made her look guilty as sin.

"I would never choose a man like you to father my child. *Never.*"

That stung, but Logan tried not to be insulted. From her point of view, he was a mercenary. That wasn't even close to what he did for a living, but to correct her would mean explaining things he couldn't get into. Best for Mia to believe the mercenary part rather than know the truth.

Some secrets should stay secret.

Not hers, of course. Because her secret involved him in the most personal way.

"So, you didn't arrange to use the semen I'd stored at Cryogen Labs?" he clarified.

"No. I didn't arrange it, and if I'd known, I would have stopped it before the insemination."

Logan continued to push because he still wasn't convinced she was telling the truth. "When did you find out I was the anonymous donor?"

Her gaze lifted slowly and met his. "When I saw your file. By then, it was too late. As I said, I was already five months pregnant."

He studied her, thought about it. She seemed sincere, but that didn't mean she was. Someone had arranged this and Mia Crandall was the most likely candidate. Maybe if he discovered her motive all the other pieces would fall into place. Which would be a good thing. Because so far, he hadn't been able to figure out much.

"Did you think if you had my baby, that you could blackmail me in some way?" he asked.

She looked at him as if he'd grown a third eye. "Excuse me?"

"Blackmail?" Logan repeated.

"And why exactly would I want to do that? I have money. As you probably know, I was the sole heir to my parents' estate and it was worth several million. I can live quite well for the rest of my life."

Yes, he did know that. "Maybe you wanted even more money. Or maybe you wanted to have some psychological hold over me because you feel I've wronged you. Or you feel that I owe you something. Maybe you're connected to someone involved in a past case that I worked on."

She huffed. "You're sounding paranoid."

He had a reason for that. "My ex-girl-friend made me paranoid about females in general. She used to like to follow me and make my life difficult."

Her chin came up. "Well, I'm not your ex-girlfriend. And I had no idea who you were before I saw the file that'd been tucked inside mine."

"You're sure?" Logan pressed.

"Dead sure. Plus, the reason I chose insemination was so I wouldn't have any moral or personal obligations—or for that matter, any contact whatsoever—with the sperm donor. That's all you are to me, Logan McGrath. *A sperm donor.* It doesn't matter if there was some kind of mix-up at Brighton. It doesn't matter what you think I've done. You have no part in my life or Tanner's life. Now, get out of my car."

Tanner.

For some reason, hearing the baby's name packed a huge wallop. Logan had experienced a similar feeling when he first held the little boy in his arms. Now, that little boy had a name. Tanner. And he was sleeping in the backseat just a few feet away.

Logan couldn't see the baby because the infant carrier seat was facing away from him. And he was reasonably sure that it wasn't a good idea for him to see his son. Not just yet, anyway. Not until he'd straightened out a few things with the boy's mother.

Who might be actually telling the truth.

And this time, Logan knew it didn't have

anything to do with her hair and mouth. Nope. She was making sense. Well, sort of. She was making as much sense as there could be in their situation.

"If you didn't set all of this up, then who did?" Logan asked.

"I honestly don't know, but it could have been anyone at Brighton. It's been all over the news about the illegal things they were doing there. Maybe that illegal activity included using DNA contributions without first getting permission from the donor."

Yeah. Logan had thought of that. And he'd dismissed it. "Someone forged my name on a release form at Cryogen Labs. That person also paid a hefty testing and processing fee to make sure the semen was still viable. It would have been a lot cheaper just to pay a new donor."

Her silence let him know that she was probably thinking about that. The silence didn't last long. From the backseat, there was a tiny sound. Like a little grunt. That grunt was followed by some movement.

And then a kittenlike cry.

Mia put her forearm over her chest. Specifically, her breasts, and pressed hard. "Tanner's crying makes my milk let down."

He didn't have a clue what that meant, and his blank stare must have conveyed that.

"I have to feed him," she snapped.

"Oh."

Well, that left him with a dilemma. He couldn't leave, not until they had this mess figured out. But the baby was obviously hungry. The kittenlike sounds increased in both volume and intensity.

And that wasn't all.

With everything else going on, Logan noticed the slow-moving dark-gray car that turned into the parking lot. Any car would have garnered his attention since the attack on him six and a half weeks earlier. But with the baby, Logan's concerns were heightened.

Really heightened.

Man. This wasn't good. He needed to view what was going on here objectively, and he couldn't do that if he was worried about the baby. Still, he couldn't totally dismiss the emotions and feelings that came with unexpected fatherhood.

Mia must have noticed his mental battle

because she followed his gaze to the gray car that was now one row over from them. "Do you know the person in that car?"

"I don't think so."

Her breathing was suddenly a little choppy. "Maybe it's your ex-girlfriend?"

"No." But he almost wished it was Genevieve Devereux. The alternative scenarios were much, much worse than running into a lying, scheming, psycho ex with a penchant for stalking.

Logan had been on the job for nearly seven years. And never once had the job come home with him.

Not until six and a half weeks ago.

Then, he'd been shot in the leg while doing target practice on Christmas morning in the woods near his former training facility.

But was the job responsible for that and had the job followed him here? Had someone associated with the mission sent an assassin to try to put another bullet in him? He didn't want to believe it was possible, but he was having a hard time coming up with theories that didn't involve his last mission.

Or Mia Crandall.

"See what you can do to soothe the baby," Logan insisted when the cries became louder. He eased his gun from his leather shoulder holster and fastened his attention to the gray car. The windows of the vehicle were heavily tinted so he couldn't see the driver. The license plate had been obscured with mud.

"Oh, God," he heard Mia say.

His attention snapped to her. She was looking at the gun and, judging from her expression, she didn't care much for it. Tough. He wasn't putting it away.

Mia drew in a series of sharp breaths and it seemed as if she were on the verge of hyperventilating. "Phobia," she managed to say through those sharp breaths.

Logan shook his head. "What?"

"Phobia. A huge one. About the gun."

She wasn't kidding, either. He could see the sweat pop out above her upper lip. She was shaking. Actually shaking. Logan had read the police report of the incident involving the death of her parents fourteen years ago. Guns had been used.

And a switchblade.

Logan rethought that part about keeping his gun drawn. He didn't want her to craze out on him. He eased his gun back inside his coat so that it would still be ready to use but would be out of sight.

"Thank you," she whispered.

Logan pushed that emotional response aside and tried to come up with a solution to this possible problem. His first instinct was to put Mia in the backseat with the baby so he could drive away. But it was broad daylight and they were outside a pediatric clinic. An assassin wasn't likely to make his or her move here.

He hoped.

"Something *is* wrong," she insisted.

She reached for her diaper bag. Without taking his eyes off the car, Logan snagged her wrist. He didn't know if she had another can of pepper spray stashed inside and he didn't want to take the chance that she might use it on him.

"I'm getting a pacifier," she informed him through clenched teeth. "I don't want to sit here in this parking lot any longer. Not with that car inching toward us like a killer shark."

Logan heard something in her voice. Not fear. But familiarity with fear. Then, he remembered her saying that she'd been followed and that someone had planted a tracking device on her car.

"How about an ex-boyfriend?" Logan asked. "Is there one in the picture?"

"No." She located the pacifier, reached over the seat and apparently put it in Tanner's mouth. It must have worked because the baby's crying stopped. "I'm leaving now. Get out."

"*We're* leaving. I'm not getting out. This isn't a good time for Tanner and you to be alone."

Mia didn't argue. She strapped on her seat belt, threw the car into gear and backed out of the parking space. She didn't waste any time. Nor did she panic. Mia drove away from the clinic, took the first turn to the right and then made an immediate turn left on the next street. She continued the process for four more blocks, all the while checking the rear-view mirror.

"You've done this before," Logan commented, staring into his side mirror. He didn't see the gray car but that didn't mean it wasn't trying to follow them.

"I told you about the problems I had with exactly this sort of thing."

Yes, she had. And it was also a matter of police record. Still, there were things that the police records didn't tell him. "What happened when someone tried to kidnap you?"

"It was…terrifying." And that's all she said for several long moments. "Early one morning when I stepped outside to get my newspaper, a van pulled up in my driveway. A person wearing a ski mask and bulky clothes came rushing out of the van and tried to use a stun gun on me. I threw the paper at him. I must have hit him or her in the eye because the person stopped. That's when I ran back inside. My neighbor saw the whole thing and yelled out for help. The person got back in the van and sped away."

Logan didn't want to know how scary that must have been. Pregnant and with someone out to get her. It was even more unsettling when he factored in that Mia had been carrying his child at the time. That meant the moron in the van had put his son at risk.

Logan intended to find that person soon.

"When did all of this start?" he asked. "When did you first notice someone following you?"

"About the time I was inseminated."

Well, that was interesting. Logan didn't think the timing was a coincidence.

But what did it mean?

"I have no ex-boyfriends. No enemies. The men who killed my parents died in a shoot-out with the cops." She made another turn and headed for the main highway. "I thought, after I learned that you were the sperm donor, that it might be connected to you."

He'd considered that, too, but he wanted to hear how she'd reached that conclusion. "How?"

"Maybe you riled the wrong person. Maybe he or she thinks they can use my baby to get back at you. Blackmail, of sorts."

"Now who's sounding paranoid?" he muttered. But he couldn't dismiss it.

"That's why I went to your brother's house in Fall Creek. I read that he was doctor, that he had a normal life. Unlike you.

He had an interview on a medical site and he said that you and he were estranged."

Because that's what Logan had told his brother, Finn, to say. It was his attempt to keep Finn out of harm's way in case one of Logan's missions went wrong and someone wanted to use his brother as leverage to exact revenge against Logan.

"I thought it would be safe to go to your brother and try to figure all of this out," she concluded. "I was obviously wrong."

"You were wrong in one way." His brother probably couldn't have helped. But if she hadn't gone to Fall Creek, Logan might have never known that he had a son.

A son who needed protecting.

Of course, there was a flip side to this. His son might need protecting because Logan had helped bring the danger right to him.

Hell.

Was this all his fault?

"I had a job a little more than seven weeks ago," he explained to her. He chose his words carefully. "A businesswoman was kidnapped in South America. Her family hired me to get her out. I did. The day after I returned to Texas, someone shot me. That's why I was using a cane in Fall Creek. I'd gone to my brother's house to recuperate."

Her breath stilled, but he could see the pulse hammer on her throat.

"I don't think my shooting is connected to you," he continued when she didn't say anything. And he hoped to hell that he was right. "After all, someone has been following you for months. So the questions are— who's been doing that and why?"

Mia shook her head, plowed one hand into the side of her thick hair to push it away from her face. "I thought maybe someone from the Brighton Birthing Center was following me because they believed I had some evidence of their crimes."

"Okay. That's possible."

"Then why follow me now?" she wanted to know. "The people who did illegal things at Brighton have all been arrested."

"Maybe not. Maybe there's a straggler."

Her eyes widened. "What does that mean?"

"Someone who was doing illegal stuff but

wasn't caught with the rest. Someone who doesn't want their illegal activity to come to light because it'll land his or her butt in jail."

She nodded. "And maybe that's the person who forged your name on the release documents and moved your file from Cryogen Labs to Brighton." She took the ramp that merged into Highway 281, a major thoroughfare of the city.

"Exactly." Logan turned his ear toward the baby to make sure he wasn't in need of a feeding. But Tanner was apparently resting comfortably.

Unlike Mia.

Logan couldn't help but notice the dampness on the front of her sweater. Right in the vicinity of her left nipple. She apparently had sprung a leak. He hoped that wasn't painful.

And then he questioned why he had his mind on that and not their situation.

Remedying that, Logan went to the next question on his mental list. "Did you ever see the person following you?"

"Once. I got just a glimpse. It happened right after I went to the police station to turn in the files I'd taken. The person was in the parking lot."

Logan hadn't read that in the police reports. "By any chance was it a dark-gray car?"

She shook her head. "Black. But the tint on the windows was heavy. When I spotted the car and realized that it was someone following me, I stopped. I figured I was safe in the parking lot of the police station so I sat there for five minutes, and then this motorcycle bumped into the black car. The driver let down the window. Just for second. And that's when I got a glimpse of her right before she sped off."

Logan latched right on to that. *"She?"*

"Oh, it was definitely a woman. Auburn hair, fair skin. Heart-shaped face."

With just that brief description, a really bad thought went through his head. "Describe her hair."

"It was short, no more than two inches long, and it was sort of spiky. She didn't look like a criminal. From what I could see of her, she was well dressed. And the car was top of the line and very expensive."

Logan silently cursed.

"What's wrong?" Mia asked. "Do you know this woman?"

He didn't answer. Because in this case a picture was worth a thousand words, he grabbed his BlackBerry from his pocket, entered a security code and began to search through the old files and photos. He finally found what he was looking for. Logan brought up the image on the screen and leaned it toward Mia so that she could see it.

"Is that the woman you saw in the parking lot that day?" he asked.

Her eyes widened and she pulled off the side of the road into the emergency lane. She took the PDA from his hand and studied the image. "Yes, I think it is. Do you know her?"

"Oh, yeah." Logan knew her all too well. "That's Genevieve Devereux, my scheming, psycho ex-girlfriend."

Chapter Three

Mia tried to come to terms with what Logan had just told her, but it was a lot to absorb.

The woman who'd followed her and made her life a living hell was Logan's ex-girl-friend?

Part of her was pleased that she finally had a name to associate with the frightening things that'd happened to her during the past year. But another part of her was confused and not at all certain that this woman was actually responsible.

There were things that just didn't add up.

"Why would Genevieve Devereux follow me and try to kidnap me?" Mia asked.

Logan didn't know the answer to that. "She's capable of doing something like this," he said. But then, he shook his head. "Well, maybe she is. I never pegged her for a kidnapper. But the subterfuge. Following you. The planting of a tracking device. That's Genevieve."

"It still doesn't explain a motive. I don't even know this woman. Besides, it could have been a coincidence that she was in the black car at the police parking lot on that particular day."

"When Genevieve is around," he mumbled, "bad things aren't usually a coincidence."

Tanner began to fuss again and Mia knew she had to feed him soon. But where? She didn't like the idea of taking Logan back to her house. Besides, she was a good fifteen minutes from home and she doubted that her son would want to wait that long for dinner.

"Take this exit," Logan instructed.

Mia gave him a questioning glance.

"Tanner's hungry," was Logan's response.

Since Mia couldn't argue with that, she did as he said and took the exit.

"Pull into the parking lot of that fast food place," he continued. "You can feed the baby while I watch out for that gray car and make some calls. I'll find out if Genevieve is behind this."

Because Tanner's cries were getting louder and more intense, Mia followed that order, too. She parked her car, unfastened her seat belt and reached for her son.

She froze.

Because she realized that Logan would see Tanner. It was stupid and it didn't make sense, but she was afraid if Logan saw the baby, then there might be some kind of instant bonding. But then, maybe that had already taken place on the afternoon he'd delivered Tanner.

After all, Logan had been the first person to hold her son.

Mia refused to think of Tanner as *their* son. No. Logan McGrath was simply the sperm donor.

Keeping the blanket over Tanner, she unstrapped him from the infant carrier, scooped him up and brought him into the front seat with her. One glance at Logan and she realized he was watching her every move. Mia had a remedy for that. She shoved her modesty aside, lifted her sweater and opened the cup clasp of her nursing bra.

Her left breast spilled out.

Logan looked away and took out his phone.

Finally she'd won one of the little mental matches going on between them.

As Mia had known he would do, her son latched right on to her nipple and began to nurse. That not only meant he was being fed, but with Tanner's face pressed to her own body, Logan couldn't see him.

Mercy, she felt petty.

But she wasn't going to blindly trust this man who'd charged into her life. Mia had made that mistake when she was fifteen. She'd trusted a stranger. And that trust had gotten her family killed and had left her a dysfunctional mess. She was not only claustrophobic, she had an almost paralyzing fear of guns and knives. It was entirely possible she would never fully trust again. And there was only one person she could blame for that.

Herself.

"I'd like to take you to my house," Logan said as he pressed some numbers on his tiny phone.

"No." And Mia left no room for argument. "If your ex-girlfriend is behind this, then your house is off-limits. For that matter, so are you."

"I own several places." He ignored her jab. "Genevieve doesn't know where this house is."

"I'm still not going there with you. After I'm done nursing Tanner, I'll make sure no one has followed us and then I'll drop you off somewhere so that Tanner and I can go home."

And once there, she would lock the door, turn on the elaborate security system she'd had installed and not go out again unless it was absolutely necessary.

Logan didn't respond to that, either. That's because his call connected. Mia heard him request "backup and a clean vehicle," and he gave the person the address of the fast food place where they were parked. He also ordered someone to go through the surveillance videos of the parking lot of the Wilson Pediatric Clinic, the place where Tanner had just had his checkup.

And the place where the gray car had first followed them.

Of course there'd be surveillance videos of the clinic. She wished she'd thought of that. It might give her some proof as to who this person was.

"Why did you request a car?" Mia wanted to know the moment he ended the call.

"There might be a tracking device on yours," he calmly answered.

Mia's reaction certainly wasn't calm. She hadn't even considered that. Yet, she should have, especially since it'd already happened once before.

"The clean car should be here in about ten minutes. We'll trade out vehicles and I'll have this one searched to see if we can find anything."

"If there's a tracking device—"

"I'm keeping watch," he insisted.

And he was. Logan had one hand on the butt of his gun, and used the other hand to make a second call.

"Logan McGrath," he greeted the person he phoned. "I need to speak to Collena Drake. No. It's important. I'll hold for her."

Mia recognized the name from the newspaper articles she'd read. Collena Drake was the former San Antonio police sergeant who was now head of the task force to uncover the illegal activity that'd happened at the Brighton Birthing Center. What Mia didn't know was why Logan was calling her at a time like this.

"Do you think Collena Drake will know something about who's been following me?" Mia asked.

"Maybe. But even if she doesn't, I still have to consider that Genevieve is in this neck-deep. Trust me, we don't want Genevieve involved even in a minor way. She's got the money and the resources to do all sorts of nasty things. But then, so do I."

The last part sounded a little like a threat. If the woman was truly guilty, Mia felt like issuing threats—and worse—herself.

"Collena," Logan greeted a moment later. "I have a problem. I've found a possible connected between the Brighton Birthing Center and Genevieve Devereux. I need to go over some things with you. Could you possibly meet me at one-twenty-seven Rosewood Drive on the north side of town? It's only about ten miles from your office."

That was Mia's address. Not that she was surprised that Logan already knew it.

Did he also know that just his mere presence was crushing her heart? She wouldn't share Tanner with him. Tanner was her life. Her world. And she didn't want anyone else in that world with them.

Mia continued to listen to his phone conversation, trying to sift through Logan's responses to see if Collena Drake could provide them with any info. But she was soon distracted from doing that. Tanner stopped sucking, and she knew he was done with his dinner. She quickly fixed her bra.

Still trying to keep the blanket over him, she maneuvered him to her shoulder so she could burp him. The movement caught Logan's attention, and he watched the process for a moment before turning his attention back to their surroundings.

Thankfully, Tanner gave a quick burp and Mia strapped him back into his carrier seat.

"Collena will meet us at your house," Logan relayed when she got back behind the wheel. He glanced back at Tanner's seat again and slipped his phone into his jacket pocket.

"You really think Collena Drake has any information about Genevieve?" Mia asked.

"We'll see. She's been studying the records taken from Brighton. There was a legal set of files, but the illegal activity was encrypted in various codes in a separate set of files. Collena's managed to break some of those codes—that's why she's head of the task force—but in some cases she has information but no names to connect to it. It's like taking dozens of puzzles, mixing up the pieces and then trying to put them back together."

Mia understood the frustration. "Do any of those pieces actually point to Genevieve?"

"Unfortunately, yes. Her father, George Devereux, was one of Brighton's main investors. He's in jail already for an unrelated crime. He claims he didn't know the clinic was shady when he put up the money."

"You believe him?"

"No. But there's no hard evidence to prove otherwise. Once I have you and Tanner settled and safe, I'll see if I can arrange a visit with my ex's father."

Mia could definitely see the benefit of

that, but it sounded like yet another involvement that she didn't want to have.

Logan turned and looked out the back window. "The police are still searching for one investor," Logan continued. "A man named Donnie Bishop. Unfortunately, Bishop has eluded them by staying at his residence in Mexico. There isn't enough evidence to extradite him, so the cops are just waiting for him to make a return visit to the States."

With every new bit of information that Mia learned, she became sorrier and sorrier that she'd ever stepped foot in Brighton. She wished she'd gone anywhere but there for the insemination.

"Donnie Bishop," she repeated.

But the man's name rang no bells. It was the first she'd heard of him and she hoped it would be the last. She didn't want anyone associated with Brighton involved in what was going on with her now. Of course, the alternative wasn't much easier to accept.

Because the alternative included a criminal, George Devereux, and his unstable stalker daughter, Genevieve.

Logan pointed to the sleek hunter green car that cruised into the parking lot and stopped next to them. "That's our clean vehicle."

Mia considered the risks of doing such a transfer, but if Logan was right, if there was indeed a tracking device on her car, then the transfer needed to happen immediately before something else could go wrong. She didn't want another encounter with that slow-moving gray car that'd been in the parking lot of the pediatric clinic. She didn't want anyone else to find out where she lived.

A man with long dark hair stepped out from the other vehicle. Logan reached over and unlocked Mia's door. Unfortunately, his arm brushed against her right breast. Mia reacted. She sucked in her breath.

"Sorry," he mumbled. "Did I hurt you?"

"No." Her reaction definitely hadn't been from pain. Odd that even though she was a nursing mother, her breasts were apparently still capable of reacting in a pleasurable way to a man's touch.

Mia pushed that realization aside.

The other man worked fast. He opened

Mia's door and Logan got out, then walked to her side of the car. She noticed the limp then. It was slight. But it was also an indication that he might not be a hundred percent healed as she'd originally thought.

The man with the long hair made the same smooth transfer with Tanner still in his carrier seat. In less than a minute Logan was behind the wheel and they were back on the road.

"That was one of your employees?" she asked.

He nodded.

She considered asking more about his job but decided it was a subject best left undiscussed. Besides, she didn't intend for Logan to be in her life for long, so there was no need for her to learn anything else about him.

"So, what do we do next?" she asked.

"We go to your house. We get Tanner inside. And we'll wait for Collena. She was going to make some calls. By the time she arrives, she might already have answers."

Well, that would help to speed things along. "Is it possible that your ex-girlfriend was also an investor at the Brighton Center?"

"It's possible. Collena has someone pouring through all the surveillance tapes that were confiscated from the center. We're talking months and months of tapes."

That was not what she wanted to hear. "So much for speeding things along," Mia mumbled.

He glanced at her. "You know you're not going to just get rid of me, right?"

She didn't want to hear that, either. "I know no such thing."

"I'm not going to leave my son—"

"He's not your son," she snapped.

Logan made a *hmmmp* sound. "Well, I might have started off as the sperm donor, but we're past that now."

No. They weren't. "I don't want or need a man in my life. That includes you."

"Then think of it this way. I won't be the man in your life, Mia. I'll be the man in Tanner's life." He paused, waiting for an objection. "You're aware that you could be in danger."

A burst of air left her mouth. Almost a laugh. But she was definitely not happy. "I'm aware of it. I'm also aware that I wouldn't be in danger if it weren't for you and your ex."

He looked as if she'd slapped him.

Mia felt as if she had, too. "Sorry. You didn't deserve that last part. I mean, we haven't even connected your ex to this."

Silence.

The moment crawled by.

Before he finally spoke. "I have a theory."

That chilled her to the bone. "What?"

More silence. "Last year, when Genevieve and I were still together, I found out that she'd been taking fertility drugs. She also tampered with my condoms."

Mia was starting to put together a mental image of this woman, and there was little about that image that she liked. "She wanted a baby."

He nodded. "It was an obsession with her. She believed a baby would bring us closer together. She wanted marriage."

"You didn't want those things." It wasn't exactly a question.

"Not with her. Genevieve knew that right from the start."

Mia believed him. Despite what he did for

a living, he didn't seem the sort of man who'd have to lie to get a woman into bed. "Did she get pregnant?"

"I don't think so. After I found the fertility drugs, we argued and she stormed out. A few days later, I got an e-mail from her saying that she would always love me but that she needed time apart so she could think. That was a little less than eleven months ago."

Around the time Mia had undergone the insemination.

"Maybe Genevieve did get pregnant," Mia concluded. "Maybe that's her connection to Brighton. She could have had your baby there."

Logan immediately shook his head. "If she'd found some way to overcome her infertility and have my baby, she would have told me. In fact, she would have been delighted to tell me because she would have thought that would get us back together. It wouldn't have. I would have taken care of my child, but that care wouldn't have extended to the mother."

Mia didn't believe that last part. After all,

he was trying to protect her, a stranger. However, she didn't have the bad blood with him that Genevieve apparently did. They only had a severe case of dislike of each other.

She hoped it continued.

Mia needed all the emotional barriers she could get to make herself immune to this man that her body seemed interested in. Because she could still feel the tingle of his touch on her breast.

Damn him.

He glanced at her and took the final turn into her secluded neighborhood. "But you're right about one thing," he continued. "Maybe that's how Genevieve is connected to Brighton."

Now, it was Mia's turn to shake her head. "I don't understand."

"Genevieve could have been the one who arranged to have the semen transported from Cryogen to Brighton. That's how she intended to get pregnant."

"And then somehow I got the semen by mistake?" Mia shook her head. "That seems like a huge blunder for a medical center to make."

"We're talking about Brighton," he reminded her. "They made a lot of mistakes. Some intentional and some because they were trying to cover up their crimes."

He took the turn into her driveway. Her house wasn't a typical burbs kind of place. Mia had bought the three-bedroom ranch-style house because of the privacy. The house was positioned amid several sprawling oaks, shrubs and hedges. Tonight, amid those oaks and in front of her house, she could see a woman.

Mia's heart started to race.

"It's all right," Logan assured her. "That's Collena Drake."

Mia got a better look at the woman when they came to a stop directly in front her. The tall, too-thin blonde seemed oblivious to the winter wind. She wore a black coat, unbuttoned, and her bare hands were exposed. The wind whipped at her shoulder-length hair and her clothes. She seemed pale and frail. As if she wasn't all there.

"Collena," Logan greeted as he stepped from the car. "I'm glad you came."

After checking that Tanner was still asleep

in his carrier in the backseat, Mia also got out, and Logan made introductions that Collena dismissed by dropping a little bombshell.

"Ms. Crandall, I've been going through the Brighton files, and I don't think the things that happened with your insemination were accidental."

Okay. Even though Mia and Logan had just played around with that theory, it was a different thing hearing it confirmed. "So, what went wrong?" Mia asked.

Collena Drake opened her mouth to answer, but that was as far as she got. Mia saw the woman's eyes widen, and she tried to figure out why Collena had that reaction.

Mia caught just a glimpse of the car out of the corner of her eye. A slow-moving gray car. The same vehicle from the parking lot of the pediatric clinic. This time, the passenger's side window was lowered about halfway. Not enough, though, to see inside the darkened interior.

Everything happened fast.

Almost a blur.

Logan yelled for them to get down. But he

didn't wait for her to comply. He dived at Mia and knocked her to ground. He didn't stay there. He came up, with his gun drawn and ready to fire.

But it was already too late.

There was a thick, heavy blast from the open window of the gray car. The brutal sound tore through the otherwise quiet community and slammed right past where Mia had just been standing.

But Mia was no longer there and the bullet hit Collena Drake instead.

And the gunman continued to fire.

Chapter Four

Logan cursed, took aim and returned fire.

He didn't stop with one shot. He sent a barrage of bullets at the gray car, all the while kicking himself for not having done more to protect everyone.

Now, Mia and Tanner were right in the path of danger and Collena Drake was down, perhaps dying.

He could blame himself for that. And later, he would. But right now, he had a more immediate problem that required his complete concentration. The gunman, or perhaps gunmen, inside that gray car could still be trying to kill them.

Logan sent two more shots into the car. One slammed into the passenger-side door, right where a gunman would be sitting if there was indeed more than one of them. The next bullet shattered the partially lowered window. The safety glass webbed into a sheet of broken pebbles and collapsed into the interior of the car.

The gunman was wearing a black ski mask.

That was the only glimpse that Logan got of the lone person shooting at them before the driver stomped on the accelerator and the car sped away.

Logan's instincts screamed for him to go in pursuit. Adrenaline and anger made him want to strike out, to retaliate, to get the SOB who'd put Collena, Mia and Tanner in danger.

But he couldn't leave them.

"The baby," Mia cried out, trying to get out from beneath him.

Logan literally had her flattened on the frozen winter ground so that she couldn't move and she obviously wanted to get up. He understood that. The baby was in the car and they had to make sure he was okay.

"The car's bullet resistant," Logan assured her.

But that didn't assure her at all. Actually, it didn't assure him, either. Nothing would at this point except seeing for himself that his son hadn't been harmed.

Keeping her eyes off his gun, Mia continued to struggle to get up and, once he made sure that the gunman's vehicle was no longer in sight, Logan moved off her. She rushed to check on Tanner.

Logan kept watch for the gray car, in case the gunman decided to return for another round, and he scrambled across the ground toward Collena.

She was alive, but bleeding from the bullet she'd taken in the shoulder. Blood had already spread across her clothes and it was hard to tell the exact point of impact, but the injury looked close to her heart.

"Tanner's okay," Mia shouted to him.

And despite everything else going on, Logan felt immediate relief. "Stay in the car," he ordered.

The bullet-resistant car would be safer than trying to get them into her house. Especially since he hadn't had a chance to check her place to make sure that no one was lurking inside. The last thing they needed was to run into another murder attempt.

He took out his phone, called 911 and requested police and an ambulance. He also called for backup from two of his own men. They'd likely get there faster than the police.

"I'll be okay," Collena mumbled.

Logan hoped that was true. Still, he didn't like what he saw when he pulled down the collar of her sweater and spotted the wound. The bullet had missed her heart, thank God, but her collarbone appeared to be shattered and she was bleeding out fast.

He took her neck scarf from her coat pocket and pressed it to the wound. "The ambulance will be here soon."

"Can I do something to help?" he heard Mia ask.

The car door was open just a fraction, enough for him to see Mia cradling Tanner to her chest. The baby was fussing, probably because his nap had been disturbed, but he looked unharmed.

Logan said a quick prayer of thanks.

"I need to get Collena to the front seat,"

he told Mia. He purposely kept his gun at his side so that she wouldn't see it and have a panic attack.

Mia nodded, reached over the seat and fully opened the front passenger-side door. Logan lifted Collena as gently as he could. She moaned and grimaced from the pain.

Logan lay her inside on the leather seat while he continued to apply pressure to her wound. It wasn't an ideal way to treat a gunshot victim, but at least the vehicle would protect them from the cold and perhaps even a subsequent attack. In the meantime, he would do what he could to keep Collena from bleeding to death.

"Are you okay?" he asked Mia.

Their eyes met. For a second. He saw the fear and concern. "I wasn't hurt."

Maybe not physically. But this attack was the stuff of present and future nightmares. It would stay with her.

And him.

The only good thing he could see in all of this was that Tanner was too young to remember what they'd just experienced.

Logan heard the sirens in the distance. It

wouldn't be long now before the police arrived and before Collena could get the medical treatment she needed.

"Someone doesn't want us to learn the truth," Collena whispered.

Logan had to agree with her about that. "We need to know who." So he could go after this idiot with every ounce of the rage he was feeling for the person who'd endangered his child.

"I'm close to getting that name," Collena added. "I'll have it soon."

"I don't doubt that we'll find the truth. But for now, just stay quiet. Conserve your energy."

Collena shook her head and ran her tongue over her chapped bottom lip. Her breath was ragged and thin. "The police found two sets of files at Brighton—the legal set the Brighton owners and investors created for the world to see. The real files were encrypted with different codes for different files. This afternoon, I finally broke the code on Mia Crandall's file."

That got his attention. Mia's, too. She peered over the seat at the woman.

"There's one notation that really stood out," Collena continued. She waited until she took a deep breath. "In Mia's file there was a notation about a surrogate request. A client paid a huge sum of money for the use of a surrogate with red hair and brown eyes. I don't know who this person is yet—they were identified by yet another code."

Logan got a really bad feeling about this.

"What was that doing in my records?" Mia asked.

Collena wearily shook her head. "I'm not sure, exactly. And it's more complicated."

The sounds of sirens drew closer and Logan spotted the ambulance when it turned into Mia's drive.

"Complicated," Collena repeated. "Because Brighton took money from both you and this other person who made the request. In fact, this person paid nearly ten times what you did, and I think the reason for that was the surrogate wasn't supposed to know she was a surrogate. The client wanted to keep the arrangement a secret."

Mia shook her head. "Why?"

"No reason given. At least, no reason that

I've been able to get from the encrypted files."

Logan groaned.

Because he knew the reason.

He knew.

MIA WAS STILL SHAKING.

Just as she'd done at the police station. And while giving her statement to the sergeant about the shooting. The shaking had continued on the ride from the police station to the hospital to check on Collena.

Of course, it'd only been three and a half hours since she'd seen a woman gunned down in front of her own house. It might take weeks before the shaking stopped and her body returned to normal.

Thankfully, Tanner wasn't having the same panicked reaction she was. He was sleeping soundly after his second nursing since the ordeal. She hadn't minded the extra feeding. In fact, Mia had welcomed it. It got her out of the hospital waiting room and into a private lounge off the nurses' station where she could finally have some downtime and try to smother the brutal images of that gunman.

Mia heard the sound of someone moving around in the nurses' station so she snapped up the cup to her nursing bra and lowered her sweater, just in case someone walked in, but she didn't put Tanner back in his carry seat. She needed to hold him a few moments longer because he was the ultimate reminder that she couldn't fall apart. Nor could she give into old fears and panic. She'd have to stay strong for her son.

She checked Tanner's diaper and discovered he was still dry. Then Mia reached for her diaper bag, so she could get ready to leave her temporary sanctuary, only to realize she didn't have the bag with her.

Oh, mercy. Not only were Tanner's extra diapers in there, so was her wallet and cell phone. She got up, searched around the fold-up chair where she'd been sitting. No bag. So she latched on to the carrier with her left hand and went back into the nurses' station. She immediately spotted the diaper bag on the floor next to the station desk.

She also spotted the pair of nurses seated at the desk, one of whom had shown her to the private lounge. The woman was now on the phone, and the other nurse was discussing something with a young couple standing directly in front of the desk. The nurses probably hadn't noticed the diaper bag because it was tucked just out of their sight.

Mia also noticed the tall, lanky man in the passageway by the nurses' station.

Even though he was dressed in green scrubs and likely a doctor or nurse, her heart went into overdrive. Simply because he was there, partially blocking her view and path, he felt threatening. It was a familiar reaction, one she couldn't totally control and she stepped back into the lounge. But he didn't even glance in her direction.

"Collena Drake will be in recovery soon?" he asked the nurse on the phone.

She checked the computer screen in front of her, nodded. "She should be on the way to the PACU in the next ten minutes or so," she said. The woman continued her phone conversation as the man walked away.

The PACU, the post-anesthesia care unit. That meant, hopefully, that Collena had come through the surgery just fine.

Mia waited to make sure the man was

gone, then cursed her wussy reaction. She couldn't keep doing this. She had to try to maintain some kind of normalcy for Tanner and that wouldn't happen if she thought of every stranger as the bogeyman.

She only hoped the shooter wasn't anywhere near the hospital. And while she was hoping, Mia added a wish that Collena Drake would be all right. She had enough guilt without adding Ms. Drake to the list. After all, the woman had been shot while trying to help Logan and her.

Mia put Tanner back into his carrier, picked up the diaper bag and went into the corridor. Logan was there at the other end, on his cell phone. He was also pacing, but he stopped when he spotted her.

"Dig deep," she heard Logan say. It was an order. "Find out how the devil this could have happened. And get someone over here now just in case the police don't put a guard on Collena Drake."

This time Mia didn't mind Logan's orders because they weren't aimed at her and because Collena obviously needed protection. They would also likely need to *dig deep* to find out what was going on. They had a lot of questions, few answers, and the answers they did have only created more questions.

"Collena just got out of surgery," Logan let her know. "The doctor should be out soon to talk to us."

He took the diaper bag and led her to the unoccupied seats on the far side of the room. She sat next to Logan and purposely put the carrier on the other side of her—away from him.

The ploy didn't work.

"Is he okay?" Logan asked, looking into the carrier. He reached over her, his arm brushing against her breasts, and used his index finger to pull back the blanket so he could see Tanner's face.

Mia moved his arm away. "He just finished eating. He'll sleep for several hours now."

He frowned, probably because she hadn't let him touch the baby. "Does he need anything?"

"No. That's the advantage of nursing. I don't have to heat formula or wash bottles.

And as for diapers, I had some with me in the bag."

This time, Logan didn't touch Tanner. He touched her. He used his finger to push a strand of hair out of her eyes. It felt... intimate.

Mia moved away again.

No frown this time. But he did put some distance between them. Logan leaned his head back against the wall and folded his arms over his chest. "What about you?" he asked. "You have to be exhausted. It's nearly 10:00 p.m."

Yes, she was exhausted. With Tanner not sleeping through the night yet, she was usually in bed by nine so she could get up for his 2:00 a.m. nursing. The fatigue was only worse with the adrenaline crash that'd hit her earlier.

"I can wait until we talk to the doctor about Collena," she let him know.

Mia owed the woman that much.

While she was waiting, she needed to figure out what she was going to do. The police hadn't offered any form of protection. They didn't have the manpower for it, they'd said when she brought up the subject. And she couldn't very well go home since her front lawn was a crime scene. With no family or close friends nearby, that left her with few options. A hotel, one with security.

Or she could ask for Logan's help.

She glanced at him. The rumpled hair. Those dark, dangerous blue eyes. The total male intensity that frightened her. Mia made her decision.

She would check in to a hotel.

Which for some stupid reason made her feel guilty. Why? Because she was shutting out Logan. But then, she didn't have a choice about that. For her own personal sanity, she had to shut him out. Yes, this situation was horrible and not of his own making. And yes, he probably thought he had a right to touch and see Tanner, but it couldn't happen.

Still, she did owe Logan something, too.

Mia cleared her throat to get his attention. "I didn't say thank you for saving our lives."

He shrugged. "We got lucky. Let's hope Collena is equally lucky." Logan glanced at her, unfolded his arms. "I had my crew go through your car and they found something."

That comment put her on instant alert. "What?"

"Someone had planted a listening device inside it, under the dash."

Mia swallowed hard and tried to prevent her stomach from churning. "How long had it been there?"

"Not long. It looked brand-new. Perhaps someone hid it in your car when you were inside the pediatric clinic. I didn't get there until shortly after you'd arrived for your appointment."

She tried to process that. It seemed like a piece of a puzzle. Only in this case, lots of pieces were missing. "Before today, I don't think anyone had been following me for the past six weeks."

He stayed quiet a moment. "That might be true. The person might have followed the same paper trail I did."

Oh. She hadn't thought of that. "And they got to my car ahead of you," she concluded.

"It looks like it." He turned in the seat and faced her. "I know you don't have any reason to trust me, but that's what I'm going to have to ask you to do."

Mia didn't like the sound of that, either. "I'm checking in to a hotel," she blurted out.

"I'd rather you not do that. I'd like to take you to one of my houses."

She was shaking her head before he even finished. "That wouldn't be safe."

"I've already told you that Genevieve doesn't know where this place is."

"So you've said. But we don't know for certain that she's the one behind the shooting. It could be someone who's tracking your every move."

Logan drew in a weary-sounding breath. "Here's what I think happened. Genevieve wanted to have a child with me because she thought it would save our doomed relationship. When she couldn't get pregnant, she put her plan into action—she broke up with me under the guise of giving herself some time to think and then she went straight to the Brighton Birthing Center and requested they immediately find her a surrogate. One who looked like her."

Mia felt her eyes widen. "Are you saying that Genevieve thought I would be her surrogate?"

"She didn't just think it. She *planned* it, and she had plenty of help from her criminal friends at Brighton. She probably paid them to be on the lookout for a surrogate like you. She would have needed someone ASAP since the baby's birth couldn't have happened much more than nine months after I last slept with her. So when you walked in the door of the birthing center, your fate was sealed."

It took a moment to say anything, but her mind was racing with the possibility and the improbability of Logan's theory. "That doesn't make sense."

Didn't it?

She didn't *want* it to make sense.

There had to be obvious massive holes in that speculation. Because Mia didn't want to think that someone could have intentionally done something like this.

Logan stood and it took a moment to figure out why he'd done that. Mia soon spotted the doctor coming their way.

"Mr. McGrath?" the doctor asked.

Logan nodded. "How's Collena?"

"She came through surgery just fine. The

bullet broke her collarbone, then exited through her back. It did some damage to her shoulder. With some physical therapy, she should be close to perfect in a few months."

Logan shook the doctor's hand. "Thank you." The breath he released was one of relief. "I'll be back to check on her, but in the meantime, if she needs anything, my number is at the nurses' station."

Mia waited until the doctor had walked away before she spoke. She was relieved that Collena was going to be okay, but they had a new issue on their hands. "I don't think your ex-girlfriend would have paid Brighton to make me a surrogate. That's insane and criminal."

"Genevieve is capable of doing insane, criminal things. She's desperate and desperate people do terrible things—including using you. I figure she planned to kidnap Tanner when he was born and then try to pass him off as the son that she herself had delivered."

"Oh, mercy." Mia pressed her fingertips to her mouth. Her doubts about the theory were starting to melt away.

"Yeah." Logan took a deep breath. "The sickening thing is her plan might have worked, too, if you hadn't come to see my brother and delivered Tanner on the porch. If I hadn't been suspicious and if you hadn't gone into hiding, I believe Genevieve would have kidnapped Tanner and brought him to me, telling me he was our baby."

Mia couldn't speak and she felt herself start to tremble again.

"Once she'd done that," Logan continued. "I would have had Tanner's DNA tested, of course, to prove he was my son. And the DNA would have proven just that. What I probably wouldn't have done was requested a maternity test. Because it wouldn't have crossed my mind that Genevieve could have done something this heinous."

"But you really think she did?" Mia asked, her voice nearly soundless.

He didn't answer her. "You can't check in to a hotel," Logan insisted. "I know it's hard, but you have to trust me to keep you and Tanner safe."

"Wait a minute." And because she needed time to compose herself, Mia repeated it.

"Genevieve must have known a plan like this wouldn't work. After all, I wouldn't have gone to Brighton if I hadn't desperately wanted a baby. I wouldn't have just stood still and allowed her to kidnap Tanner. I would have fought—"

Her gaze flew to Logan's. She could see the confirmation in his eyes. A confirmation of what she'd just realized.

He reached out, slowly, and slid his arm around her. He pulled her to him. Mia didn't resist. She was too numb and sick to resist.

"Genevieve would have killed you and taken Tanner," Logan supplied. "And I think that's what she still plans to do."

Chapter Five

Logan unlocked the door to his north-side San Antonio home and disengaged the security system so that Mia, Tanner and he could go inside.

He'd won the first battle with her. Thank God. He'd convinced Mia to go with him to his house, but it was obvious she wasn't happy with the decision. She had a white-knuckle grip on Tanner's carrier seat, and she eyed the place as if it were the enemy's camp.

Which was no doubt the way she felt about it.

To her, he was the enemy. He was the last man on earth she would have chosen to father her baby. Plus, in the hours since their second meeting at the pediatric clinic, she'd been followed, shot at and forced out of her own home.

And also during that time, Mia had learned the reason that someone likely wanted her dead.

That was a lot for anyone to deal with, especially since the threat wasn't over. In many ways, it'd just begun.

"Here's the guest room," Logan said, leading her through the Mexican-tiled kitchen and to the other side of the house.

The place wasn't grand by anyone's standards, but it had a homey feel to it, thanks to the decorator he'd hired. Everything was designed for comfort because it was his place to get away from it all. Nestled on the Guadalupe River amid four acres, it was still technically within city limits. Close enough to the city but also the perfect place for peace and quiet.

He hoped.

Logan flipped on the lamps in the guest room, set the diaper bag on the floor and turned back the earth-toned log cabin quilt on the queen-size bed. He did a quick scan to make sure the curtains were drawn and the tiny red security lights next to the windows were on, meaning the windows were locked and secured. Not that he had thought differently. Someone he trusted from his team had already checked out the entire house and grounds to make sure it was as safe as it could possibly be.

"There are pj's in the dresser that might fit you," he whispered so he wouldn't wake the baby. "And you should find a toothbrush and some toiletries in the bathroom. If you're hungry, just help yourself to anything in the kitchen."

She gave a crisp nod.

"There's obviously no crib," he continued. "But I've arranged to have one delivered in the morning. Extra diapers and baby clothes are on the way, too."

"That's not necessary," she practically snapped. "We won't be here that long and Tanner can sleep in the carrier tonight." She sat it on the center of the bed and turned back around to face him.

Logan heard the argument they were going to have before she even spoke a word. So he tried to diffuse it and alleviate some of her fears. "I'm not trying to worm my way into your life."

Her mouth was already open, but that closed it. Temporarily. "It feels that way."

"I know. And I wish I could change that, but I can't. I need to keep Tanner safe until we can figure out what's going on. And since you're breast-feeding him, and since you're his mother, you're stuck here with him. For *his* sake," Logan added.

He considered adding *for your sake, too,* but he instinctively knew that would only cause her more concern. Heck, it would cause him concern, as well, because his focus had to be on Tanner, not Tanner's mom.

But he *would* get to know his son, and would be a father, even if that hadn't been Mia's plan from the start. Now that he knew about Tanner, he couldn't go back and extract himself from the picture.

Mia huffed, but that simple sound seemed to take the wind out of her sails. Or maybe she was just too tired to argue. Logan certainly was.

"Genevieve might not even be behind the

shooting," she said, rubbing her fingertips over her left temple. Obviously she'd given this some thought on the thirty-five minute drive from the hospital to the house. "We don't even know if we're looking in the right direction."

"Genevieve isn't the *only* direction," Logan agreed. "She's just a start. I also have my people looking for Donnie Bishop."

"The man you mentioned earlier? You said he was an investor at Brighton," Mia supplied.

"Did you ever meet him?"

"No."

"I doubt he spent much time around the clients or patients. From what I can tell, he dealt with the criminal elements. Anyway, if he knew about your forced surrogacy, he could be trying to cover his tracks so there won't be anyone to testify against him."

Still, Logan's first choice of suspects was Genevieve.

Tanner stirred inside the carrier and Logan tried to bend closer to check on him, but Mia stepped in front of him.

That probably wasn't the best idea she'd ever had, because her attempt to stop him resulted in them landing against each other, breasts against chest.

There it was again. That kick. His body reacted to her. A reaction that Logan shoved to the side.

What he didn't do was move. Nope. Even if they had to stand there all night, he was going to see his son. He only hoped he didn't have to stand there all night. He was tired and, worse, he was physically reacting to the contact with Mia.

Mia reacted, too. He saw the pulse jump on her throat. Though that probably didn't have anything to do with attraction. At least he hoped it didn't. It was for the best that only one of them was going insane. If they both did, it was going to cause one helluva distraction that neither of them needed.

Their eyes met.

And held for what seemed an eternity.

The pulse on her throat jumped again. She moistened her lips. And she blinked. Before she finally moved to the side.

"Thank you," he mumbled, though he couldn't be totally sincere. His voice no doubt reflected his frustration. It was going to be a long battle for him to have any rights as a father.

Still, the battle would be worth it.

Logan stared down at his son. He was so little. Yet that tiny face and body stirred the deepest emotions that Logan had ever felt.

"I didn't have immediate plans for fatherhood," he admitted.

She folded her arms over her chest. "You don't have to plan on it now."

He tossed her a glance to let her know that wasn't an option. "My love for him is already there. It's unconditional. Total. Complete. I'm not just going to turn away and pretend he doesn't exist."

Mia didn't say a thing.

"He looks like me," Logan added, daring her to challenge that.

The silence lingered a while longer. "Yes."

Logan couldn't help it. He smiled. He didn't want to know how difficult it was for her to admit that, even though she had choked on the word.

"He has your hair," she whispered. No choking sound that time. Just a lot of concern and even some fear. "Your eyes."

"Your mouth." He looked at her to confirm that. But it wasn't just a look.

They shared…something.

Something that only parents could share. Their merged DNA had made this precious child. That was normally preceded by an intimate sexual act.

But Mia and he were strangers.

Strange.

Even though they'd never really touched, because of Tanner they were forever bonded in the most intimate way. And that intimacy brought with it a whole host of concerns.

Mia, for one.

He felt…things for her. Feelings and desires that stirred deep within him. It was some kind of transference. Because she was the mother of his son.

And that was the only explanation Logan intended to accept.

But then he shook his head. It was a sad day in a man's life when he started lying to himself. What he felt for her wasn't transference.

It was lust.

She was beautiful and he was attracted to her.

However, lusting after Mia was only part of his list of concerns. He had to keep her alive. He had to prevent another attack. He had to deal with her animosity. Her fears.

And then, there were his more immediate concerns for his son.

"Tanner's okay, right?" Logan asked. "I mean, the pediatrician didn't notice anything wrong?" With everything else that'd gone on, Logan hadn't even remembered to discuss the six weeks' checkup.

"He's very healthy."

"Good. After the way he started his life…" Logan didn't finish that. Because even if Genevieve had any part of this, she still hadn't contributed to Tanner's DNA.

Mia stepped closer, so that she was right next to him. "I just thought of something. Something a little sick. If Genevieve has done what you think she has, then she's ultimately responsible for Tanner's conception."

"Yeah." Fate really had a sense of humor. "But she doesn't get a gold star for that. If I'm right about her, then her motives weren't merely to create a child but to create one she could use to manipulate me."

Mia actually cringed. It was nauseating to think of how Genevieve would have treated Tanner once she had what she wanted. The manipulation and lies would have continued and Logan seriously doubted that she would have been much as a mother.

"I didn't go back to my house after I delivered Tanner on your brother's porch," Mia said.

"Because you thought I'd follow you there." Logan knew where she was going with this. "But it might have saved you from Genevieve or whoever was following you."

She nodded. "I went into hiding again. I'd set up an emergency cash fund and I used that. No credit cards. No paper trail. Or so I thought. I probably should have left the state, or the country."

Logan was thankful she hadn't, because he might have never found his son. But if she had left, then Tanner and she would have been safe.

His phone rang and when Logan glanced at his cell screen, he saw that the call was from Jason Cartwright, one of the P.I.s who worked for him. "Tell me you have some good news," Logan greeted the man. He stepped out of the guest room so that the conversation wouldn't wake Tanner.

Mia followed him into the nearby kitchen.

"No good news," Jason explained. "All I have is information that may or may not be helpful. I just came from Mia Crandall's house. The crime-scene folks didn't find anything, and none of her neighbors could give even a sketchy description of the person inside the gunman's vehicle."

Logan cursed under his breath. He hadn't really expected an eyewitness account that would lead to an arrest, but he had hoped that someone at least thought they saw Genevieve in that car. Without that, the police wouldn't have enough to get a search warrant to go through her house and vehicles.

"Did the police bring Genevieve in for questioning?" Logan wanted to know.

"They did, just about a half hour ago. She had her lawyer with her."

"Royce Foreman?" Logan asked.

"That's the one. You know him?"

Logan tried not to groan too loudly. "I've

met him. Foreman is a former lover and very devoted to her. He couldn't stand the sight of me, and I'm about certain that he's not only in love with Genevieve, he'd do anything for her."

Jason thought about that. "You believe he could have been the gunman in that car?"

"It's possible. I hope the cops will swab his and Genevieve's hands for gunshot residue."

"I'll make sure they do."

But both the P.I. and Logan knew that if the shooter had worn gloves, then there would not be any evidence of the residue.

"If Royce Foreman was the shooter, then this might be important," Jason continued. "Before the shooting, you asked us to check out the surveillance videos of the Wilson Pediatric Clinic. I had a team do that and we saw the person who put the bug in Mia Crandall's car. It happened right before you got there."

Well, the good news was that he hadn't led this person to Mia, but that didn't give Logan much comfort. The person had likely followed an obvious paper trail of pediatric appointments. And that meant anyone could have done it.

"You have a photo of the person who planted the bug?" Logan hoped.

"No. The person was wearing bulky clothes and kept turned away from the surveillance camera. It was obvious that he knew about the security and didn't want to be recognized."

So, it could have been Genevieve. Or not. With her money and resources, she could have hired someone to do the job.

"What about the vehicle the person used?" Logan asked. "Did you get anything from that?"

"No. But there might be something else. I went back through several hours on the surveillance tapes, and I saw someone in the parking lot about three hours before Ms. Crandall's appointment with the pediatrician. The person seemed to be checking out the place, then he parked one building over."

Oh, he did not like the sound of this. *"He?"* Logan questioned.

"It was definitely a man. And no ski mask.

But I don't think it's the same person who put the bug in Ms. Crandall's car."

Logan didn't like the sound of that, either. Was it possible they had more than one person after them?

"Was this other man driving the gray car?" Logan asked.

"No. A white SUV. There's no clean image of the license plates so I can't run them. The man stayed there in the adjacent parking lot until after you arrived, and then it appears he followed you and Ms. Crandall when you left the scene."

Logan cursed again. He'd been so damn preoccupied with the gray car that he hadn't even noticed the white SUV.

"I took a still shot from the surveillance video," Jason continued. "I'm sending a photo over your cell. See if you recognize him."

Logan looked at the screen and loaded the picture. It took a moment for the grainy shot to appear in full, but it wasn't so grainy that he could see the man who was lurking around the parking lot. And the guy was definitely lurking—everything about his body language suggested that.

Mia moved closer and had a look as well. "I've seen that man before."

"Yes. So have I. Well, I've seen another picture of him, anyway. That's Donnie Bishop. He's obviously back in the country."

What the heck did Bishop want, and was he the person who'd tried to kill them?

Logan put the phone back to his ear. "Find Donnie Bishop," he instructed Jason. "Take him to the police, but I want to talk to him, too. Listen in on his conversations before and after he's at the police station. I want to know what he's up to."

"Will do, boss."

"That's Donnie Bishop?" Mia asked almost frantically when he ended the call.

Logan looked at her and saw the renewed panic in her eyes. "It is. Where have you seen him?"

Mia swallowed hard. "He was at the hospital when I was nursing Tanner."

Because of her reaction, he slipped the phone into his pocket and caught on to her shoulders. "Did he threaten you or something?"

"No." Her eyes widened. "But he asked

about Collena Drake. He wanted to know where she'd be taken after surgery. And the nurse told him."

Hell.

Logan grabbed his phone to call the hospital. He already had one of his team in the corridor outside the recovery area, but that might not be enough.

He only hoped he wasn't too late.

Chapter Six

Mia lay in the bed of Logan's guest room and listened to his phone conversation. Something she'd been doing for the past half hour.

Even though he was in the kitchen, she could hear snatches of what he said. Mainly, though, she could tell from the calm tone of his voice that everything was okay with Collena.

His tone was in direct contrast to the calls he'd made the night before when they'd realized that Donnie Bishop had been at the hospital. Then, Logan had made a flurry of calls to the police and his team so that security could be provided for Collena.

Thankfully, the security hadn't been necessary.

Donnie Bishop hadn't shown his face again anywhere near the hospital and especially not near Collena's room. Mia figured the man had seen one of Logan's team members and had decided not to make a second attempt.

But that left her with questions.

Did that mean Donnie Bishop was after Collena and not her? Or maybe Bishop had no part in the shooting. Maybe he was there at the hospital for other reasons.

But what would those be?

Mia didn't know, but she figured all of this was connected to the Brighton Birthing Center.

Tanner stirred, finishing his breakfast. That was Mia's cue to burp him. Despite the fatigue headache and her not-so-rosy outlook for the immediate future, just holding Tanner close made her feel better. She kissed his cheek, then changed his diaper.

It was the last one in her bag, which meant she'd need a fresh supply within the next two hours.

Looking down at the bulky navy-blue pj's,

she realized the same was true for her. She didn't even have a change of underwear.

She'd have to ask Logan to get some things for her.

Mia was already dreading that. She hated relying on him, even though she knew she had no choice. Tanner had to come first and, whether she liked it or not, Logan would definitely protect Tanner.

With the baby nestled into her arms, she walked to the door. Mia resisted stopping by the dresser mirror to check her appearance. For reasons she didn't want to explore, it was best that she looked her worst when she was around her "host."

Mia found Logan in the kitchen. He had the phone sandwiched between his ear and shoulder and he was making breakfast. Scrambled eggs, bacon and toast. The toast popped up the moment he turned in her direction.

Mia took a deep breath.

She'd braced herself for his possible reaction to her less-than-stellar appearance, but she hadn't braced herself for *his* appearance. No black suit this morning. He was barefooted and wore faded jeans and a plain white cotton tee that seemed to accentuate every muscle in his body.

He wasn't bulky like a bodybuilder, but it was obvious he spent time working out.

It was also obvious that her body responded to that mouthwatering physique in a basic, female kind of way. Fortunately, her common sense calmed that reaction.

However, a different kind of feeling returned when she spotted the laptop on the counter. Logan had apparently been surfing the net for baby information. The page on the screen was titled Your Baby's First Six Months.

That riled her. How could she stop Logan from wanting to be part of Tanner's life? But Mia already knew the answer to that.

She couldn't.

Logan said goodbye to the caller, slipped his phone into his pocket and tipped his head to Tanner. "Is he awake?"

Mia glanced down to confirm what she already knew. "Not quite. He's still in that newborn stage, which you probably know means he sleeps a lot."

"Yeah." He glanced at the computer screen and then back at her as if trying go gauge her reaction. "I read that. Lots of sleep. Nursing every three to four hours."

"That means lots of diaper changes, too. And he's out of them. I could use a change of clothes, as well."

"They're on the way. One of my team collected some things from your house and is bringing them over."

"Oh. Good." Though it made her uncomfortable to know that someone had gone through her house.

"Is that okay with you?" He proceeded to dish up two plates of food.

Mia shrugged. "I'm a private person."

"So I gathered." He deposited the plates on the table, along with some silverware and glasses of orange juice. "Is that because of what happened to your parents?"

She sat at the table when he did. "I suppose." She changed the subject. "How's Collena doing this morning?" Mia preferred that subject to anything personal about Tanner or her.

"Better." He glanced at Tanner when the

baby made a small sound. "I still have guards at the hospital and they'll stay there until I'm sure she's safe."

"How long will that be?"

"Hopefully not long. I have team members who'll have a chat with Genevieve and her lawyer, Royce Foreman. Oh, and the police managed to pick up Donnie Bishop."

Mia certainly hadn't expected that to happen so soon. "Really? They found him?" That helped her stomach settle down a bit.

"Yep. Near the hospital. They cuffed him and put him in lockup, but so far he's refused to say anything. He did make one phone call, though. Not to his lawyer, either. To Genevieve."

"They're friends?" Mia asked, surprised.

"More like acquaintances."

"So, maybe she called a lawyer for him." Mia nibbled at the piece of buttered toast. "And maybe Donnie was after Collena, because she's the one who could uncover evidence to send him to prison. He could have been the gunman in the car."

Logan sipped his juice and made a sound of agreement. And just like that, that particular conversation seemed to be tapped out. The room went silent.

Uncomfortably silent.

Mia suddenly became aware of how intimate it felt to be sitting in Logan's pj's, in his kitchen, eating breakfast that he'd prepared. She also noticed Logan glancing at Tanner again. Her feeling of discomfort went up a significant notch.

"I'll get his carrier," she said, standing.

Much to her surprise, Logan didn't get up, as well. In fact, he sat there, studying her as she went into the narrow hall and then the guest bedroom. She took several deep breaths before she put Tanner in the carrier and went back into the room. She sat the carrier on the floor next to her.

Still, Logan didn't say anything, though it was clear from his intense gaze and bunched up forehead that he had something on his mind. He sat there, ate some eggs and finished off his juice.

Maybe that was his tactic: no conversation. Make her totally uncomfortable. Grill her with that stare. And then she'd start blabbing.

Which is exactly what she did.

"I haven't let you hold Tanner yet because, frankly, I'm scared of you," Mia heard herself say. She groaned, knowing she should have never opened up this subject for discussion, but unable to put it off any longer. Her ten-pound, eleven-ounce son was the equivalent of the six-hundred-pound gorilla in the room.

Logan made another sound of agreement. "You still think I'm a mercenary."

"Aren't you?"

He calmly got up and poured himself some coffee. He offered her a cup by lifting the carafe, but Mia declined, shaking her head.

"I do special rescues," Logan explained, returning to the table.

But he didn't just return, he repositioned his chair so that it was closer to both Tanner and her. Logan leaned back, practically lounging, his long legs stretched out in front of him.

"Define special rescues," Mia insisted.

"I didn't think you'd want to know that."

She shook her head. "I don't really want to, but…"

He waited a moment and the corner of his mouth lifted. Almost a smile. "But you know that you should learn everything about me because I'm Tanner's father."

"His biological father."

"His father." There was some bite to his tone. "And I'm not the slimy criminal you think I am."

"Yes, because you do special rescues," she mumbled, her sarcasm showing through.

No more lounging. He sat up in the chair as if preparing for some kind of official briefing. "My team is contracted by the government when they need a quiet rescue."

Still skeptical, she shook her head. "And what exactly is a quiet rescue?"

"Let's say that the U.S. Department of State wants businesses, perfectly legal ones, to be established in a country where we have little or no diplomatic relations. And then let's say something goes wrong, like the head of the company is kidnapped. The government wouldn't want the word to get out about the kidnapping. That's literally bad for business. And they can't send in the military. Too much publicity. No CIA, either. Too much flak if the international press gets wind of it."

"So, they hire you?" Mia asked.

"They hire me," he confirmed.

It sounded legitimate. But there was still the obvious objection. "Okay, so maybe I was wrong about you being a mercenary. But I wasn't wrong about the danger. Do you really think with what you do that you could be a suitable father?"

"Funny you should mention that. Two months ago I would have had my own doubts about fatherhood. But this injury changed everything."

Mia was so surprised that it took her a moment to ask her next question. "You're changing your line of work?"

"Yeah. Out of necessity. Rescue agents need to be a hundred percent. I'm not. And my leg never will be. My top employee, Jason Cartwright, will buy the company, and I'll concentrate on a new venture—bodyguard services."

Oh, she didn't like this. Without that dark, dangerous cloud hanging over him, Logan might actually seem to be more…human.

And fatherly.

"Personal security can be risky, too," she pointed out.

"Not as much as you obviously hope it will be."

She frowned at his smugness. "But it still could be dangerous."

"Not really. I'll run the company from my laptop. Or this house," he said, using his cup to motion around the room. "But I don't want to get into a footrace with some badass who can outrun me because of this bum leg."

Mia searched for another objection. There had to be one, but it didn't immediately come to mind. "You're certain that the injury is permanent?"

He nodded, sending Mia's pulse and her fears galloping out of control. Because of Logan's injury and his future job plans, she could no longer have any career objections to his fatherhood.

But she sure as heck could have other objections.

"I wanted a baby," she said. "I planned to have one. I never planned on having a father in the picture because I'm not much of a relationship person."

She hated that she sounded a little hysterical, even irrational, but damn it, her well-planned life was falling apart—again.

"I'm sorry." He sounded genuine, leaned closer. So close that she caught his scent—spicy deodorant soap and a musky, manly aftershave. "I wish I could make you feel safe."

Safe?

That wasn't it. That wasn't why she objected to him.

Or was it?

Just like that, she was fifteen again and all those horrible images and thoughts came flooding back. Her life had been almost perfect then. Plans for dating, college and travel. She had a phone book filled with friends' numbers.

And then, she'd blown it.

"I don't think anyone can make me feel safe," she admitted and hated that her voice actually cracked.

He reached out and slid his hand over hers. "You weren't responsible for what happened to your parents."

It was an old argument, one she'd heard

dozens of times. An argument she'd never been able to believe. "I met those two boys at the mall that day. I was attracted to one of them. Because he had that whole bad-boy, biker attitude. We talked. I flirted, a lot. I invited him over." Mia had to pause a moment. "He came and brought his friend with him. And then later, he came again. That time he broke in."

Logan sipped his coffee and studied her. "You think because you flirted with him and invited him to your house that you contributed to the crime?"

"I know I did. If I hadn't invited him, he wouldn't have been there."

"You don't know that. He was a killer. He might have targeted you the moment he saw you in the mall. He might have come after you even if you hadn't flirted with him."

"There are a lot of *mights* in that." Because she couldn't bear his intense gaze any longer, she looked away. "But I'd love to believe it. I'd love for the nightmares and phobias to stop."

She moved her hand from his. Because she thought it was a good idea. Because she couldn't do this. She couldn't let these little heart-to-heart talks soften her feeling toward him.

"I don't usually talk about this," she said. "With anyone."

Logan nodded, leaned back in his chair and lounged again. "Then I feel privileged that you talked about it with me."

Alarms went off in her head. They told her to take a huge step away from him. "I won't make a mistake like that again. I won't ever be attracted to another dangerous man."

He just stared at her with those heavy-lidded sizzling-blue eyes. She figured those eyes alone had been responsible for many seductions. They were certainly responsible for the sudden warmth she was feeling.

"All right," she finally said. "I'll *try* very hard not to be attracted to a dangerous man."

And for some crazy reason, that confession made her smile. Sweet heaven, it was stupid. She'd just admitted to Logan that she was attracted to him and that was the last thing she should have done. That information in his hands could be very…dangerous.

Her smile was short-lived. But not the attraction. Mia could feel it—simmering, growing. Oh, yes, it was growing, even though she knew it shouldn't.

But she couldn't stop it.

Logan obviously couldn't, either. He shook his head, as if trying to clear it, but that didn't work. Because he leaned in. Toward her. She caught not just his scent, but she got an even closer look at those eyes that were creating a frenzy inside her.

He was frowning when his mouth came to hers.

Mia could feel that frown—along with the other things. The jolt of pleasure. The sensation of being kissed by a man who knew how to do it right. No pressure. No intrusion. Just the touch of his lips to hers.

For just a few seconds, she forgot all about the danger. She forgot that he was the enemy who could ruin her plans for the future. She forgot about everything.

Everything, but Logan.

Mia just let herself…feel. She let the heat of the pleasure slide through her. For those few seconds, she didn't allow the old fears to win out.

Still, she hadn't gone completely insane, either. Mia pulled away from, forcing herself to stop.

When she opened her eyes, she could see that Logan was still frowning. She was certain that she was frowning, too.

And then she heard the sound.

A car approaching the house.

Logan and she jerked away from each other as if they'd been caught doing something wrong.

Which wasn't far from the truth.

That kiss shouldn't have happened. No way. She was playing with fire and, in this case, the fire could cost her full custody of her son. But the car was a more immediate concern. No more passionate haze. No more thoughts of kisses. Her body went on an alert of a different kind.

The gunman could have found them.

"It's probably one of my men with the supplies," Logan assured her.

Oh. She'd somehow forgotten about that. Obviously, she'd forgotten a lot of things— like common sense and the consequences of doing something stupid.

While she chastised herself, Logan took his holster from the top of the fridge and went to investigate. Mia could see him looking out one of the side windows that framed the door.

Mia also saw the immediate change in his body language.

"Take Tanner and go into the bedroom," he ordered. He hurriedly put on his boots, drew his gun and used his cell phone to call for backup.

That didn't do a thing to steady her nerves. "What's wrong?"

"That's not my team member out there. It's Genevieve Devereux and her lawyer, Royce Foreman."

Chapter Seven

How the hell had Genevieve found them?

That was the foremost question on Logan's mind as he watched the car come to a stop next to his SUV.

One thing was for certain, he'd never brought Genevieve or Royce to the house. He'd never even mentioned the place to either of them. And on the drive from the hospital the night before, he'd taken a circuitous route to make sure no one had followed Mia and him.

And no one had, he was positive of that.

Yet, here were Genevieve and her lawyer friend stepping from a sleek red sports car as if they had come to pay a friendly visit.

Logan knew there wouldn't be anything friendly about it.

Both his visitors were wearing coats. They'd both probably come armed. Genevieve was partial to carrying a snub-nosed .38 in her purse, and Logan had learned from a background check that Royce had a permit to carry concealed.

Logan was prepared to take them both out if they so much as reached for a gun. He wasn't going to put Tanner or Mia at any more risk, and he would use every ounce of his training to make sure they stayed safe.

He checked to see that Mia had taken Tanner to the bedroom. She had. What she hadn't done was close the door all the way. She was peeking out, probably waiting for him to assure her that all was well.

He couldn't do that just yet.

Genevieve walked just a few steps ahead of her lawyer, and had her attention focused on Royce rather than the house. They appeared to be arguing or at least having an intense discussion about something. Neither seemed on the verge of pulling out semi-automatics and launching an attack.

But Logan prepared himself just in case that happened.

Genevieve kept her pace at a leisurely stroll. Maybe because she was wearing bloodred stilettos and it was difficult to walk on the frozen ground. Whatever the reason, it gave Logan plenty of time to observe her.

She certainly hadn't changed in the past year. The same short, choppy red hair. The same aristocratic demeanor. She was as high maintenance as they came. Once, Logan had been able to overlook that, but that was before she showed her true colors. With the lies, drama-queen episodes and obsessive behavior, he'd learned that she was not worth the price of that high maintenance.

However, there were some changes in Royce Foreman. Worry lines creased his forehead and there were threads of gray in his otherwise dark-brown hair. Logan was betting that unlike the man's cashmere coat, the gray wasn't there to make a fashion statement. Genevieve was likely responsible for Royce's aging.

When the couple was within ten feet of the porch, Logan disengaged the security system, threw open the door and took aim at them.

"Don't come any closer," he warned.

The pair stopped, but if either of them had any fear of his weapon or his thoroughly riled expression, they didn't show it. They both stood there, staring at him.

Logan glared right back at them.

"The police came to my home and interrogated Royce and me," Genevieve announced, adding a little huff. "They talked to us as if we were common criminals." She shoved her kid-gloved hands into the pockets of her expensive duster-length black coat. Anger flared in her cat-green eyes. That anger also tightened the muscles in her face.

Royce Foreman wasn't faring much better. There was lots of anger there, too, and it was obvious from the way he had his arm looped around Genevieve's waist that he was being territorial. Perhaps even protective.

"How did you find this place?" Logan demanded.

"Did you hear me?" Genevieve countered, not answering his question. "The police interrogated us."

"They should have arrested you."

Genevieve's crimson-red mouth tightened even more. She took a step toward him. Logan lifted his gun to readjust his aim. That was apparently enough to stop her from taking another step.

"Genevieve and I did nothing wrong," Royce declared. "You have no right to treat her this way."

Since Genevieve's hands were in her pockets, and therefore perhaps on her gun, Logan kept his main focus on her. "You did nothing wrong? You didn't orchestrate an involuntary and therefore illegal surrogacy deal at the Brighton Birthing Center?"

Genevieve flinched, as if he'd slapped her. "I'll tell you the same thing I told the police—no, I didn't."

"She had no reason to do that, Logan," Royce supplied. He was still glaring; the winter wind was causing his otherwise pale, Nordic face to redden. "It was over between you two. Genevieve had already walked out on you when all of that happened at Brighton."

That last part was true, but because Logan was watching Genevieve so closely, he could see the longing still in her eyes. She might not still be madly in love with him, perhaps she never was, but he recognized that look. And he didn't think he was mistaken that she wanted him back.

What he couldn't see in her face was guilt.

It was odd—Logan had been certain he would see it. Genevieve wasn't exactly an expert at hiding her feelings. Of course, maybe she'd developed a poker face in the past year.

"Are you saying you didn't follow this surrogate from Brighton after she was impregnated?" Logan asked.

Ah, now there was some guilt in her eyes. It was followed by an admission when Genevieve nodded. "I did follow Mia Crandall, but only because I couldn't figure out what was going on. I thought she might have some answers."

Logan hadn't expected her to say that. "What do you mean?"

"Someone was following me, too," Genevieve insisted, jerking her hand from her pocket and flattening it on her chest. "And yes, I'd gone to Brighton to inquire about hiring a surrogate—"

"So you could produce our baby," Logan interrupted.

Again, there was some guilt. Her cheeks reddened, as well, but it could have all been a result of the icy February wind. "Yes, but I changed my mind."

Logan gave her a flat look. "Did you?"

Genevieve's chin came up. "Yes. I didn't go through with anything other than the initial payment. But when I realized someone was following me, I went to Brighton and demanded to know what was going on. I got a look at the computer records and that's when I realized that they'd assigned Mia Crandall as my surrogate."

"And why would they do that if you'd cancelled the request for a surrogate?" Logan asked, still giving her that skeptical look.

"The director said someone else had paid for the remainder of the fee and requested that the surrogacy continue as planned."

She seemed sincere. *Seemed* being the operative word. "Who would do something like that?" he pressed.

She shook her head. "I don't know."

"Guess," Logan insisted.

She huffed and glanced down at the frozen ground. What she didn't do was answer for several moments. "Maybe Donnie Bishop."

Again, she'd surprised him. He motioned with his gun for her to continue. However, it wasn't Genevieve but Royce who spoke for her.

"This might be linked to Genevieve's father," Royce explained.

Logan cursed under his breath. He didn't want to hear that. Nor was he sure it was true.

Better yet, he prayed it wasn't true.

He didn't want any of this connected to George Devereux. George had been another of Brighton's big investors, but he was a lot more than that. He was a dangerous criminal who was thankfully behind bars for extortion and other unsavory crimes.

"Her father knew how upset she was about her breakup with you," Royce continued. "He also knew how much she wanted a baby. We think he might have continued the surrogacy process even after Genevieve called everything off."

It didn't make sense. Well, not normal

sense, anyway. But this was George Devereux they were discussing, and from what Logan had learned about the man, he was capable of just about anything.

But this?

Why would Genevieve's father possibly want her to have a child with an ex-lover? Especially an ex-lover he'd never even met?

Logan wasn't ready to take George Devereux off his list of suspects, but he wasn't at the top of that list, either.

Genevieve was.

"How did you know where I was?" Logan asked. "And this time, don't evade the question."

"I hired a P.I.," Genevieve admitted.

She said it so quickly and so confidently that it didn't appear to be a lie.

But Logan didn't believe her.

Because, simply put, there were no records that linked him to this house. And that meant the most likely explanation for Genevieve finding him was that she or someone had managed to plant another tracking device on Mia. His team had found the one in Mia's car, but there had to be another. That was the only explanation that made sense.

Well, either that or George Devereux or Genevieve had managed to buy off someone on his team.

Logan's stomach tightened. If that was the case, he was not going to be pleased to discover a traitor in his midst.

"So now that you know the truth," Royce went on, "you can call off the police. I don't want them knocking on either of our doors again, understand?"

"As long as you're suspects—and, trust me, you are suspects—I'm sure the police will knock anytime they want."

"But I'm innocent," Genevieve declared. "I didn't go through with the surrogacy and I didn't have anything to do with that woman being shot."

"I don't believe you," Logan told her. "And the police don't believe you, either. That's why they questioned you."

Royce took a protective stance in front of Genevieve. "If you don't drop these insane accusations, I'll file a lawsuit against you for slander."

"That's the best threat you can manage?" Logan didn't wait for an answer. He looked Royce right in the eyes. "Okay, now it's my turn. If you two don't stay away from Mia Crandall and her baby, I'll personally drag you into the police station myself. Then, I'll assign my entire team and every friend I have in the United States Department of Justice to make sure you're convicted."

"I'm innocent," Genevieve repeated, though this time there was some intense emotion in it. She didn't exactly stamp her foot on the ground, but it was close.

"Leave now," Logan ordered as he slammed the door.

He then locked it and engaged the security system in case the duo had brought body-guards or gunmen along with them. He didn't want anyone sneaking up on them or trying to break in.

"I heard," Mia said coming out of the bedroom.

Logan kept watch through the side window. He also kept his weapon ready in case Royce and Genevieve decided to linger around the place. And that's exactly what they seemed to be doing. They were standing in his front yard talking.

"As soon as our visitors are on their way, get the baby," Logan instructed Mia. "But don't bring anything else with you. We have to leave."

Mia walked closer to him and he could hear the unevenness of her breathing. "You think they found us because of another bug?"

"Probably, because no one followed us here last night."

"What about the supplies?" she asked. "Maybe Genevieve followed the guy that brought them?"

Logan hoped that wasn't the case, but just in case, he took his cell phone from his pocket and called Jason Cartwright. "Please tell me you weren't followed," Logan said when Jason answered.

"No. I left San Antonio about an hour ago and have been driving all over the city to make sure no one's tailing me. Why? Did something happen?"

"Oh, yeah. Genevieve Devereux and Royce Foreman are here at the house. They came to discuss their pleasure at being interrogated."

Thankfully, Royce and Genevieve got back into their car. What they didn't do was drive away.

"Well, they didn't follow me," Jason insisted.

"That's what I figured. Mia and I are leaving within just a few minutes. When you get here, scrub down the place to see if there are any bugs."

"Will do. I'll be there in about ten minutes, maybe less. By the way, where will you go?"

"I'd rather not say over the phone." But Logan had a place in mind. He had to do something to get Mia and Tanner out of danger. And right now, Genevieve and Royce were two people that he considered very dangerous.

Logan ended the call and looked at Mia. She was a little pale, but she wasn't trembling with fear, even though his gun was clearly in sight.

"I'm sorry," he told her.

"This isn't your fault." She tipped her head to the door. "And, according to them, it's not their fault, either. Do you believe them?"

Logan was about to give an unequivocal no, but he just didn't know. Genevieve had been convincing.

"I'll find the answers," Logan assured her.

Logan reached out and gently touched her arm. Mia didn't back away. In fact she stepped closer, until she was side-by-side with him. She looked out the window.

"What if it was her father who did this?" Mia whispered.

He didn't want to consider the possibility. But he couldn't put his head in the sand. "George Devereux loves his daughter. He would have gone through with this if he thought it would make her happy."

"Then how do you explain the gunmen?"

"It's a stretch, but maybe Devereux realized the baby wouldn't make Genevieve happy after all. And maybe now he's trying to cover his tracks so that he doesn't get more jail time added to his sentence."

Mia drew in her breath and Logan could feel the muscles in her arm tense. She'd already been through too much and Logan wanted to put an end to at least what was causing her this immediate stress.

"I'm going out there to coax our guests into leaving," he informed her.

Mia caught his arm. "You think that's a good idea?"

Logan had already started to reach for the button to disengage the security system, but that stopped him. No. It wasn't a good idea, even if it'd feel damn good to try to pound some sense into Royce. But if he left the house, he'd leave Mia and Tanner more vulnerable.

Maybe that's what Genevieve and Royce wanted him to do. Leave, get distracted with a fistfight, then they would sneak someone in through the back.

"I'll wait until Jason gets here before I go out there," Logan assured her.

She nodded.

So, the concern and discomfort from their unwanted visitors would have to continue. For a while longer. But once Jason arrived, Logan would have the backup he needed and nothing would stop him from getting rid of Genevieve and Royce.

"What about Tanner's carrier seat?" she asked. "Can I bring it with us?"

"You'll have to leave it behind."

And that riled Logan, because that seat was necessary for Tanner's safety. Still, it wouldn't be beneficial to Tanner's safety, or Mia's, if Royce, Genevieve or a gunman used a tracking device to find them.

He heard Royce start the engine to his car and Logan saw the white fog from the exhaust as the heat collided with the colder air. Finally, they were leaving. He watched as the tires kicked up gravel and dirt, and he didn't stop watching until the car was out of sight.

But Logan didn't have much time to revel in the small victory of having Royce and Genevieve off his property because Logan's SUV suddenly exploded in a thundering ball of fire.

Logan caught Mia and dragged her to the floor. It wasn't a second too soon because the debris crashed through the windows and daggered through the house.

"Tanner," Mia cried out.

Logan did a quick visual check of the damage. There was broken glass and some shards of what was left of his vehicle, but none of the glass or shards had penetrated the door or walls of the guest room.

Still, that visual check didn't soothe his fears or raw nerves. Both Mia and Logan jumped up from the floor and raced toward the baby. Logan threw open the door and saw Tanner sleeping peacefully in his carrier, which Mia had positioned in the center of the bed.

His son hadn't been harmed.

Logan's relief was instantly replaced by the rage of what'd just happened. Were Royce and Genevieve responsible for this? Or had the explosive device been set prior to their arrival? He wasn't sure, but he intended to find out.

He hurried back to the window to keep watch. What was left of the SUV was in flames; black coils of smoke lashed through the air. What Logan didn't see was the culprit. It would have been awfully ballsy of Genevieve or Royce to set an explosive right in front of him, especially since one slight malfunction would have blown up her car as well.

"This has to stop," Mia said. She had a still-sleeping Tanner cradled in her arms.

Logan reached out and pulled her to him. "It will." Though he had no idea how he was going to keep that promise. And to make matters worse, he now had another suspect to consider in all of this.

George Devereux.

But Logan knew one thing—George Devereux wouldn't have risked his daughter's life by putting her in the vicinity of a bomb. Of course, it was possible that Devereux didn't know that Genevieve would be making a trip out to Logan's house.

Logan saw a team car approaching and he checked to make sure the driver was indeed Jason Cartwright.

"Let's go," Logan told Mia. He disengaged the security system and opened the door. "We're leaving now."

She swallowed hard. "Is it safe to go out there?"

"Maybe not. But we don't have a choice. If someone planted a bomb in the car, he or she could have planted one outside the house."

Chapter Eight

Because there wasn't anything else to do, Mia occupied herself by glancing around the squad room of San Antonio Police headquarters. It was better than the alternative: thinking about what'd happened at Logan's house.

She figured if she could keep her mind on mundane things like the headquarters, it might give her body a reprieve from the adrenaline spikes and flashback memories she'd been experiencing.

So, Mia forced herself to study the squad room. She looked at and listened to the little details. And the big ones. The sea of cluttered desks, ringing phones and the dozens of conversations going on all at once. Harsh fluorescent lighting. Prison-gray floor tiles. The place smelled like disinfectant and stale coffee.

This was her second visit to the headquarters in less than forty-eight hours. Mia hoped it would be her last for a long time.

As part of her job as a victims' rights advocate, she was familiar with the police station and even knew some of the officers. She'd worked closely with several of them on various cases of sexual assault and spousal abuse. However, that didn't make her feel more at ease. She was ready to get out—now. She was tired, hungry, and she felt clammy and uncomfortable.

Tanner, on the other hand, seemed perfectly content with the surroundings. Since she'd changed him, he'd been awake for nearly a half hour, his deep blue eyes tracking various people as they walked past. He watched as Logan exited the captain's office and came walking back toward them.

Logan's expression was hard and etched with frustration and fatigue. At least it was until he saw Tanner. Mia saw the change in him immediately. Logan managed a smile as he sank down in the chair next to them.

"He's awake." Logan touched the baby's cheek, and Tanner smiled, too.

Logan's expression softened and she could see the frustration and fatigue just melt away. She knew how he felt because the same thing happened to her whenever she looked at her son.

Their son, she mentally corrected. Even though there was still a part of her that wasn't able to accept that.

She'd planned her life, and Tanner's, around having no father in the picture.

Well, Logan was obviously not going anywhere.

"Some people believe that babies this age don't really smile," Mia explained. "It's just a reaction to gas."

"He's smiling."

Mia had to agree with him.

Logan looked at her. Their eyes met. And there it was again—that magnetism that kept pulling her to him. Mixed with the sexual attraction and the spent adrenaline, it was a potent combination.

Especially now.

And no amount of concentration on

mundane things like squad rooms would diminish it.

She cleared her throat and tried to clear her mind. "How soon before we can leave?"

"The captain is looking over our statements and making some calls. He wants to try to find out if George Devereux is involved."

Yes. George Devereux. The pieces to this puzzle kept multiplying, and the only pieces that fit were the ones that spelled out the potential for an even more dangerous situation. Mia didn't want Genevieve's criminal father involved in this.

"The crime-scene guys and my own team are still at the house," Logan explained. "They didn't find another bomb, thank God, and they're collecting the pieces of the one that took out the SUV."

"What about our things? Did they find a tracking device?" she asked.

"Nothing yet, but it'll take a while to go through everything."

She didn't doubt it. Mia also didn't doubt that Logan's crew and the police would be thorough. They'd already taken all their clothes for examination and had replaced them with whatever they'd been able to find in the headquarters building. Tanner was now wearing a blue T-shirt many sizes too big and Mia was dressed in gray sweatpants and a men's white button-down shirt.

The clothes made her look like a homeless person.

Logan had fared far better in the clothing department. Jeans and a snug black tee. The items fit him as if they'd been tailor-made for his body. Which was too bad. Because they only made her notice his body even more.

What was with this attraction? Yes, Logan was hot. He had that whole dangerous bad-boy thing going on. But she'd resisted men like that in the past. In fact, she easily resisted them because they triggered the old memories.

But she wasn't having such an easy time resisting Logan.

"How are you holding up?" Logan asked.

As he'd done before, he slid his hand over hers, touching both Tanner and her at the same time. And as before, alarms went off in her head. This time, she ignored the alarms.

It was true that Logan and she were getting closer, but she wasn't going to refuse his help.

Or anything else he was willing to offer.

Mercy. She hoped those great-fitting jeans didn't have anything to do with this.

"I'm okay," Mia said, and she was surprised that for the most part it was true. Instead of dwelling on what had already happened, she was far more interested in thinking about what was in their immediate future. "Where will we go when the captain lets us leave?"

Logan glanced around to make sure no one was nearby. "My team is making the arrangements. We'll go to a hotel for a while. It'll be more like a safe house when my team's done setting up the security."

She preferred a hotel to returning to either of their houses, especially since the shooting at her place and the explosion at Logan's, but she had to wonder if the new temporary living arrangements would assure them any safety whatsoever. Of course, they couldn't stay camped out in the police station, either. They had to go somewhere to regroup and figure out their next move. That's what their would-be killer was almost certainly doing.

Mia checked her watch—it was already past noon. She checked the captain's door again. Still closed. That antsy get-out-of-there feeling was building with each passing minute. Plus, she had a slight dilemma.

"Is something wrong?" Logan asked.

Because this couldn't wait, Mia put her discomfort aside and just told him, "I need to go to the bathroom and I don't have Tanner's carrier seat."

Mia knew what the solution had to be because there was only one other person in the building that she trusted with her baby.

"I need you to hold Tanner," she clarified. "I can't carry him while I'm using the bathroom." She stood and eased the sleeping baby toward Logan.

He looked surprised. Correction, he looked stunned, especially as she placed the baby in his arms.

And Mia's heart was beating fast. The concerns she had certainly hadn't faded. But there wasn't any feeling of panic at seeing Tanner's birth father holding him, and that troubled her in an entirely different kind of way.

"He's *really* little," Logan mumbled.

"Yes," she said around the lump in throat.

The scene in front of her was…confusing, to say the least. It warmed her from head to toe to see Logan so content. It made her want to get close to him. Mia wanted more than handholding. She wanted Logan.

"The last time I slept with a man, it was really awful," she heard herself say. And she groaned. Mercy. Where the heck had that come from? Fatigue and the need for a bathroom break had obviously turned her into a chatterbox.

Logan blinked. "Awful traumatic or just awful bad sex?"

And he was serious, too.

There wasn't even the hint of a smile on his handsome face.

"Awful bad sex," Mia mumbled. "I shouldn't have brought that up." She was about to make some excuses for her chattiness, but Logan spoke before she could.

"It was the guy's fault."

Because she hadn't expected him to say

something like that, it took a moment to sink in. "W-what?"

"It was the guy's fault," he calmly repeated. Then, he aimed those hot blue eyes at her and the impact of his equally hot looks hit her with full force. "Because sex with you could never be awful."

For a moment she was just too astonished to say anything. She stood there, mouth open. Yes, her mouth open. Unable to speak and not knowing what to say even if she could have somehow managed to get her mouth to form words.

The corner of Logan's mouth hitched, and he chuckled. "You know I'm attracted to you. And no, it's not because you're the mother of my child."

Mia had just been about to point that out.

"And it's not just because we're in a dangerous situation together," Logan continued. "I'd be attracted to you even if there wasn't any danger. You're a beautiful woman. But I'm also attracted to your vulnerability. And your strength."

"I'm not strong."

He shook his head, disagreeing. "You

haven't even shed a tear after two attempts to kill you. You've faced fears. And you've done all of that while taking care of a baby. I'd say that's strong. Those are the reasons I want you naked and in my bed."

The image of that stole her breath.

There was nothing she could say to that. Admitting that she would like nothing more than to be naked in his bed would be playing with fire. Especially since Logan and she were going to be spending a lot of time together.

Mia motioned toward the bathroom. "I won't be long." And she made a hasty exit before she could say something that she would ultimately regret.

She went into the ladies room, used the facilities and then splashed some water on her face. "What are you doing?" she asked herself as she stared into the mirror.

But she knew the answer.

She was developing a major case of the hots for Logan.

Despite what he'd said, he *so* wasn't her type, she reminded herself. Tall, dark and dangerous. He could also only be insinuating himself into her life for Tanner. Then, there was the part about his lethal job description.

On paper, Logan McGrath was the worst possible match for her.

Too bad her body said otherwise.

Now, she had to contend with the image of herself naked in his bed. And he'd be naked, too.

How would it feel to be taken by a man like Logan?

How would he taste?

And just how memorable of an experience would it be?

She didn't have to guess at the last question. It would be memorable, and would likely spoil her for any other man.

Disgusted with herself—and aroused— Mia dried her face and tried to put on a steely expression before she went back into the waiting area. What she saw when she returned, however, took away the steel and arousal, and the alarm and concern reappeared.

Logan was standing, holding Tanner, but he wasn't alone. There was a man in a brown uniform. The emblem above his chest pocket said Dependable Deliveries. Judging from Logan's stance, she didn't think this was something to do with his security arrangements.

The man tried to hand Logan a small caramel-colored cigar box.

Which Logan didn't take.

Instead, Logan motioned for one of the officers to come over and examine it. That alarmed her even more and Mia hurried to take the baby so she could move him away from that box and whatever was in it.

"Stay back," Logan warned her the moment she took Tanner.

Sweet heaven. She prayed it wasn't another bomb, and she stepped back into the recess of the ladies' room so that Tanner would be protected. Logan took things one step further. He used his body as a shield.

The officer examined the box. First, visually and then with a small device that a lieutenant handed him.

"It's okay," the officer concluded. He opened the box to reveal some cigars.

Mia let out the breath that she didn't even know she'd been holding.

"There's a note," the officer added. He extracted it from the box and took it to Logan.

"Congratulations on the birth of your son," Logan read aloud. "It's signed George Devereux."

That probably should have sent a shock of fear through her, but it didn't. Instead, it infuriated her. Was this some kind of mind game? If so, she wanted to throttle Devereux for keeping her on this emotional roller coaster.

"Why would he send something like that?" Mia asked.

"I don't think it was to wish us well."

No. In fact, it felt like a warning. But what kind of warning? Did Devereux want them to back off from accusing his daughter? Was that it?

Or was something else going on here?

Logan passed the cigars and the note back to the officer. "You might want to keep this in case it turns out to be evidence in the investigation," he explained.

In other words, Logan didn't want it with

them if there was another bug. But he didn't want to discard it, either, in case it contained some kind of clue.

"I'll tell the captain that we're leaving," Logan assured her.

But Logan barely made it a step in that direction. He stopped when he noticed a man making his way toward him. Mia recognized him from his photo and from her brief encounter with him at the hospital.

Donnie Bishop.

He wasn't dressed in scrubs, nor was he wearing the dark outfit he'd worn when he was skulking around the pediatric clinic parking lot. Today, he was dressed more like a rock star with fashionably ripped and faded jeans, a bright purple shirt and a dark-green leather jacket.

Mia stepped away with Tanner in case there was an altercation. Judging from Logan's body language and expression, that was a strong possibility.

"Logan McGrath," Donnie greeted. "And Mia Crandall. We meet at last."

His tone and posture were cavalier. In fact, everything about him was cavalier, down to his multiple ear and eyebrow piercings and his shoulder-length heavily highlighted blond hair. With at least five carats of diamonds winking in his ears, Donnie certainly didn't look like the sort who'd try to gun someone down, but Mia wasn't about to give him the benefit of the doubt.

"I just finished my little chat with the boys in blue," Donnie volunteered. He had a small plastic container of pellet-size breath mints, and he calmly funneled some into his mouth. "I take it you're here for the same reason?"

Logan fired off some questions of his own. "What were you doing in the hospital last night? Did you think you'd try to finish off Collena Drake?"

Donnie crunched his breath mints. "I have no interest in Ms. Drake. She's no longer a cop and, from what I understand, she's just a couple of steps from being in the loony bin."

"Someone stole her newborn baby and tried to kill her—twice—once right after she gave birth and again in front of Mia's house. With her security-tech skills, she could be earning a six-figure income, but instead she volunteered to work on the task force to find illegally adopted babies. So, have some sympathy."

"Please." Donnie made a show of rolling his eyes. "I don't have sympathy for cops, former cops or for anyone who works for the authorities on a regular basis. That would include you, McGrath."

"The feeling is mutual." Logan took a step forward. "So, what were you doing at the hospital asking about Collena Drake?"

Donnie only smirked.

Mia thought back to that night and it didn't take her long to come up with a theory. "I think I know why he was there." She stared at Donnie. "Did you put some kind of tracking equipment in my son's diaper bag?"

No more smirks, but he did seem to be amused that she'd figured it out. "Is that where it ended up? I'd been looking for the darn thing. It must have fallen in the bag accidentally."

"Accidentally?" Logan repeated, his voice practically a growl.

"Of course. I'd never put it there on purpose. I got it for a friend who wanted to keep tabs on his teenage daughter. I had it with me when I was visiting someone at the hospital, and I obviously dropped it."

"You expect me to believe that?" Logan countered.

"Believe what you will. You have no proof otherwise."

No. But there was enough circumstantial evidence to at least suggest it. But right now, they had more important issues.

"I want to know about Genevieve. Did she really put together a surrogacy plot that involved me?" Mia asked.

"You bet." He fluttered his perfectly manicured nails toward the interrogation room. "And because I wanted to do my civic duty, I just told the police all about it."

Mia was relieved that the police now knew about Genevieve, but it made her sick to her stomach to hear the confirmation that the woman had indeed planned this.

But was it true?

"Genevieve was going to steal the baby?" Logan asked.

"You're right again. And don't believe that part when she says she changed her mind, that she didn't want to go through with the surrogacy. She had every intention of going through with it, but then Ms. Crandall went into labor early, and Genevieve couldn't find her."

Mia pulled Tanner even closer. "You could be saying all of this to save yourself."

"Could be." He smiled. "The boys in blue probably think that, as well. And that's why I cut a deal with them. Not blanket immunity exactly, but they wanted information about the Brighton clinic. I'm sure you remember I was an investor, and I thought I could trade information about Genevieve so they'd be more *lenient* if there are any charges related to Brighton. I don't want to see the inside of a cell."

He'd cut a deal. Even though she barely knew this man, she wasn't surprised. She only hoped his information did indeed lead to the truth.

"Speaking of jail," Logan continued. "What about Genevieve's father? Is he involved in this?"

For the first time since they'd started this bizarre conversation, Donnie seemed to get serious. "George Devereux wouldn't do this." He tipped his head toward Mia and Tanner. "He'd just find a ready-made kid and buy it. Surrogacy is too messy."

"Maybe." Logan stepped even closer to the man. "But what if George and Genevieve wanted to make certain the child was mine so that Genevieve would have an emotional hold over me?"

"Look." Donnie's voice lowered as if he was telling a secret. "I'm not saying that George is a choirboy, but a word to the wise—leave him out of this, McGrath, because you've got enough problems without irritating Devereux. Besides, this stinks of Genevieve. Or else her lap boy, Royce Foreman." Donnie smiled again. "Now, there's a piece of work. Maybe Royce is the one who put all of this together, and just maybe Genevieve is telling the truth about trying to put an end to the baby surrogacy plan."

Logan stared at him. "And you're telling the truth now? Why?"

"Because of the deal with the cops. And if you know the truth, you'll get off my back and jump onto Genevieve's. I have enough people digging into my business without you doing it, too." He flashed another of those oily grins and aimed his eyes at Mia. "By the way, you got lucky. Because Genevieve's original plan was to smother you in your sleep after you delivered, and take the kiddo."

Mia tried not to react. She kept a stern face. Kept her chin high and her shoulders squared. But it created an emotional firestorm inside her to hear the confirmation that someone had wanted her dead. Still, she had to consider the source, who just might not be very reliable.

Donnie tried to walk closer to her, but Logan blocked his path. The man still spoke to her over Logan's shoulder. "Watch your step, though. Genevieve might still want to send you to the hereafter."

Mia shook her head. "Genevieve has no reason to kill me now."

Donnie's smirk returned. "You don't know her."

Obviously riled, Logan caught the man's arm and maneuvered him against the wall.

It was definitely a threatening posture. "What does that mean?"

"It means Genevieve just might kill you both so she can win. Without the two of you and Collena Drake to testify against her, Genevieve might believe—in her twisted little mind, of course—that there won't be any evidence against her. And that's not too far from reality. The police don't have a solid case because they don't have any proof."

Donnie leaned in and put his mouth close to Logan's ear. "But I do," Mia heard him say, though his voice had very little sound.

Logan caught a handful of Donnie's purple shirt. "What kind of proof?"

"The good kind. I carry a tape recorder everywhere I go, and if people start saying things that might be in conflict with the law, I record it. It's the best way I know to cover my own butt."

Logan waited a moment before he rammed his hand into Donnie's jacket pocket and extracted a tiny recorder. "I want those recordings," Logan insisted. "The ones that prove Genevieve's involvement."

"I'm sure you do want them—badly. What are they worth to you?"

Logan tightened his grip on Donnie's shirt and shoved the man harder against the wall. It drew the attention of one of the nearby officers, but Logan gave the man a reassuring nod that all was well.

"What are the tapes worth to you?" Donnie paraphrased. "I don't mean money, either. Let's just say I need your connections."

Logan seemed disgusted with that. "I'll have the cops get a search warrant—"

"They'll never find them. But you, on the other hand, have a wonderful opportunity to hear your ex-girlfriend in action. All you have to do is talk to your buddies in the D.A.'s office. I know you have connections there, including a former employee who used to do special-ops stuff for you. I want to make sure the cops don't renege on their *assurance* to keep me out of jail."

"I have no pull with them, and even I did, I wouldn't use any favors on you."

Donnie made a *hmmm* sound. "Too bad. Having these tapes could ultimately end the threat to the lovely Ms. Crandall and her wee babe. Or should I say *your* wee babe?"

Logan slammed Donnie so hard against the wall that it knocked the breath from him. This time, several officers came running.

"What's going on here?" a sergeant demanded.

"This piece of slime needs to be reinterrogated," Logan explained. "Ask him about recordings he made that are pertinent to the investigation. And while you're at it, have your boss rethink the deal you made with him."

The sergeant hesitated a moment before he latched on to Donnie's arm. "All right. Come with me."

"I won't give up those tapes," Donnie whispered so that only Mia and Logan could hear. "The offer is only for you, Logan McGrath. You scratch my back, and I'll give you what you need to keep Mia Crandall and your little boy alive."

Chapter Nine

While he waited on hold for Jason to return to the phone, Logan showed Mia around the suite of the Plaza Rio Hotel. The two rooms and bath would be their temporary home until he could figure out what the hell was going on.

That could take a while.

So far, he hadn't had much luck confirming the person responsible for putting them in a position where they had to hide out. Donnie was the obvious culprit because of the bug, but that didn't mean he'd been the one to try to kill them.

Logan wondered if Mia had realized that she'd be in close quarters with him indefinitely. He'd certainly given it some thought and hoped like the devil that he could first and foremost keep her safe.

Secondly, he hoped that he could keep his hands off her. Because the close quarters would be sweet torture.

"You and Tanner can sleep in here," he said, directing her into the bedroom. The bassinet and baby supplies were already in place. They had everything they needed to lay low for at least a week. "The view's great, but you'll need to keep the drapes closed."

She nodded and went to the window to peek out. Logan already knew what she would see because he'd checked out photos that Jason had e-mailed him earlier while they were still at police headquarters.

Their gilded cage was a twenty-seven-room, five-star hotel centered in downtown San Antonio, a city of more than a million people, and it was right on the River Walk, a major tourist area. All that bustle and activity seemed contradictory to security, but Logan had booked the entire hotel. And he'd had guards posted at each end of the hall and in front of the elevator.

No one was getting into the suite.

For extra security, Logan had told the hotel manager that they would be staying in room

201, but just in case the manager couldn't be trusted, they were actually staying at the other end of the hall in 208. Logan hoped the precaution wouldn't be necessary.

"This must be costing you a fortune," Mia mumbled.

"It's worth every penny."

Logan went to her and eased her away from the window. Man, she looked exhausted. He was about to insist that she take a nap when Jason came back on the line.

"I got the information you need," Jason informed him. And since some of that information might be disturbing or unsettling to Mia, Logan decided to listen to it first and then give her the sanitized version.

"I'll take this call in the sitting room," Logan told her, and for some reason, he kissed her cheek. Not a lustful kiss, either. It was more like a husbandly peck.

He hadn't even known he was going to do it before his mouth brushed against her warm face, and he didn't know which one of them looked more surprised.

Logan made a hasty exit into the adjacent room, and he went to the desk by the window, as far away from Mia as he could get. This way she wouldn't be able to hear his conversation or he would be able to get that husbandly peck off his mind. He asked Jason to continue.

"First, George Devereux," Jason started. "Over the past year, he's had multiple meetings with his daughter, but the prison guards can't say if the two were planning anything illegal. There certainly isn't any kind of paper trail to prove they were. Or to prove anything."

"What about a meeting? Did Devereux agree to see me?" Logan checked out the window and saw the trail of people strolling along both of the cobblestone sides of the River Walk. Even though it was winter, there was a crowd.

"He did. Ten, tomorrow morning at the prison. But there's a problem. He wants Mia to come, too."

Logan dropped the curtain and groaned. "Why?"

"Devereux says he wants a chance to talk to both of you about all this surrogacy stuff."

"Because he wants to try to convince us that his daughter is innocent."

"Probably. But he says the meeting won't happen unless Mia is with you."

Logan's first instinct was to refuse to bring her, but he needed answers and Devereux might be able to provide them. Still, there was no way he wanted to put Mia through something like that.

"I'll think about it," Logan told Jason. "What about Donnie Bishop? Any luck finding those disks he claims he has?"

"Not yet, but the police are getting a search warrant."

Which would probably be useless. Donnie wouldn't have mentioned them if they weren't out of reach of the authorities. He had no doubt hidden them away.

If they existed at all.

"We did find the tracking and eavesdropping device that Donnie Bishop put in Tanner's diaper bag," Jason continued. "It was identical to the one we found on Mia's car."

"Keep a tail on Bishop," Logan told Jason. "I want to know where he goes and who he sees."

"Are you going to do as Bishop asked and talk to the police about the investigation against him?" Jason wanted to know.

"As much as it riles me to think of doing it, it's possible." Heck, anything was possible, because he was going to do whatever was necessary to solve this case. "It might be a small price to pay to get actual physical evidence that the police can use. Of course, he could be lying."

"Well, he's almost certainly the one who planted a bug in the diaper bag and on the car. It's not much of stretch to think he'd plant other bugs that could have recorded incriminating conversations."

That was true, but Logan had to wonder just how much it would ultimately cost to get those recordings. He didn't mind paying Donnie money, but he didn't like the idea of helping a slimeball like that with a get-of-jail-free-card deal. Someone should have to pay for all the havoc that went on at Brighton. Even if Bishop wasn't guilty of helping Genevieve, he'd certainly been privy to some of the illegal activity going on at Brighton.

"I've arranged for a nanny-bodyguard,"

Jason continued. "Her name is Dorien Novak. I know her personally, and her references are impeccable. If you need her, all you have to do is phone me. I have her in one of the rooms on the bottom floor of the hotel, but I can move her anywhere you want."

"Thanks again." And Logan was ready to end the call so he could give some thought to what he was going to do about visiting George Devereux.

"There's more," Jason announced. And that was all he said for several moments.

That long pause caused Logan to groan again. "What's wrong now?"

"Remember Ellen Danita, the Texas businesswoman you rescued in South America right before Christmas?"

Logan instantly tensed up. Of course he remembered the owner of a coffee-processing plant who was taken hostage just before Christmas—someone had shot him within hours of his return from that rescue. "I remember Danita. Among lots of other things, her rescue was my last mission. She was taken hostage by an extremist environmental group. What about her?"

"Well, she has an old foe she believes might have orchestrated her kidnapping."

"Is it George Devereux?"

"No. Royce Foreman."

Logan didn't like this particular surprise. "Why did all of this come to light just now?"

"Because Ellen Danita only recently put two and two together and called me about it. It seems that Royce wanted to buy her shares of a business. She refused to sell. Ms. Danita speculated that Royce orchestrated the kidnapping so that she'd be murdered and her shares would come up for sale."

"Any truth to it?"

"Yeah, unfortunately. I talked to some people who said that Royce was well past being furious when you went into that jungle and brought Ms. Danita back. Her family and the Department of State had written her off as dead."

Logan considered that a moment. "Was Royce Foreman furious enough to have shot me?"

"According to my sources, yes."

So, there it was. Royce apparently had his own agenda for murder.

Logan took that piece of information and put it together with another request. "Check and see if Royce has any experience with explosives, then examine his bank accounts to see if you can find payment for a hired gun."

Jason assured him that he would and Logan ended the call. Nothing he'd learned had been good news and now he had another dilemma. He had to decide if he could dare ask Mia to go with him to see Devereux, a man who might possibly want to kill them both.

Logan drew in a weary breath and peeked out the window again. He took a moment to glance in all directions, looking around in case a sniper was on one of the balconies of the hotel directly across from them.

When he was reasonably satisfied that there was no immediate danger, Logan headed back toward the bedroom to check on Mia and have the conversation with her that he was already dreading.

He tapped on the door. No answer. So he tapped again. By the third tap his heart and imagination were racing with all sorts of bad scenarios. Logan drew his gun from his slide holster at the back of his waist and he barged right into the room.

Only to find Mia and Tanner lying on the bed.

The sound of his entry must have startled her because she rifled to a sitting position. And that's when Logan realized she'd been half asleep and nursing the baby.

She'd lifted up her top to expose her right breast.

Logan felt like a pervert because his concern instantly turned to arousal.

"What's wrong?" Mia asked. She yawned and rubbed her eyes.

Her attention landed on his gun. Just like that, she went from startled and confused to looking more than a little panicked. Logan quickly put the gun back in his slide holster so that it was out of sight.

Her breath was so rapid now that her chest was pumping. "I'm nearly thirty years old. I've been through hours of therapy, hypnosis—you name it. And I still can't make this fear of guns go away."

He walked slowly toward her. And he took a deep breath. "That's because you went through a horrible nightmare to get to where you are now. A phobia seems natural, considering everything that happened."

"You've been shot before," she pointed out, dragging her hand through her hair.

"Several times."

"And you don't have gun phobias."

"No. But that's because I've been around guns all my life. I've had a lot of training and more than a lot of experience carrying a weapon."

Logan reached down and eased her bulky top over her exposed breast.

Her eyes widened to the size of saucers, and she blushed. "Oh, sheez. I'm so sorry. I fell asleep and forgot I was nursing him."

"Don't be sorry. You just gave me fuel for fantasies."

And he wasn't joking.

Because he needed something to do with his hands—touching her wasn't an option— he lifted the sleeping baby and put him against his chest. As he'd seen Mia do. So that he could burp him. It didn't take much, just a few soft pats on the back, and his son let out a loud belch. Logan couldn't imagine a sound of that volume coming from such a tiny body.

Mia and he shared a smile, even though hers was tentative. That probably had something to do with the fact that she was still blushing.

Since he needed to have a serious conversation with Mia, he put the sleeping baby in his new bassinet. He checked the window again, something he'd no doubt be doing a lot, and then he walked back to the bed where Mia was still lying.

Did he even have the right to ask her to visit Devereux? Or was Devereux's request some kind of ploy to get Mia out in the open so that she'd be an easy target for Genevieve?

Logan sat down on the bed beside her.

"You look…intense. Is this about you seeing my breast?" she asked before he could say anything. The blush was still there on her cheeks and she was nibbling on her bottom lip.

Logan suddenly had the urge to nibble on her lip, too.

But he couldn't put this conversation off

since he had to make a decision about keeping that appointment with George Devereux.

"I've really made some missteps," Mia supplied. "First talking about the awful sex. Then, not remembering—"

"Trust me, I was thinking about having sex with you long before you brought up the subject."

Because he was so close to her, he saw the pulse jump on her throat. It was another jolt to his libido. Of course, anything she did at this point, including breathing, caused him to want her even more.

She shook her head. "Some men are really put off by the sight of a woman nursing a child."

"It didn't put me off."

Her nerves were right there at the surface. "Some men are put off after seeing a woman give birth," she tried again.

"I guess some men are."

Logan didn't see it that way. Delivering Tanner was the most incredible thing he'd ever done or ever would do. He couldn't possibly be disgusted or put off by that.

Logan knew it was a mistake, but he looked at her face.

With her hair all mussed and her eyelids heavy, she looked like the answer to some really raunchy dreams that he'd been having.

He made another mistake. He reached out and skimmed his thumb over her bottom lip. She didn't flinch. Didn't have any adverse reaction. But her breath shivered a little.

She shivered.

And that was the only invitation he needed to kick the intensity of the situation up a notch.

Logan took things slow, so she'd have an out if she wanted it, and slid his hand around the back of her neck to draw her closer to him.

Her skin was warm and soft. Welcoming. And she made a slight sound of pleasure when he lowered his head and kissed her.

The kiss was a mistake, too.

But he didn't care.

In that moment, the only thing that seemed to matter was tasting Mia. So that's what he did. Logan took his time, savoring her and letting her own unique taste slide through every inch of his body.

She put her arms around him. First one, then the other. And she eased closer to him, until her breasts touched his chest. Again, Logan waited, to make sure he wasn't breaking too many rules, but Mia broke some rules of her own. She deepened the kiss and pulled him to her.

"We shouldn't be doing this," she mumbled.

"No, we shouldn't. Do you plan to stop?"

Her answer was in her kiss, hot, long and French. Just the way he liked kisses. But the problem with really good kisses—and these were good—was that soon his body wasn't content with just mouth-to-mouth contact.

His body wanted more.

Mia's, too.

She kept inching closer and closer until she was plastered against him. Until she was seeking the physical contact that would not only make them burn hotter but also give them some release.

However, despite her hungry kisses and the way she was digging her nails into his back, this wasn't the time for sex.

Logan repeated that to himself.

And he forced himself to repeat the reasons, too. She'd just come away from a horrible ordeal and she wasn't thinking straight.

"We shouldn't be doing this," he said, restating her earlier comment.

"We've already established that."

But it didn't stop her. Heck, it didn't stop him, either. He continued to kiss her. And touch her. He slid his hand along her waist and then her hip.

Mia moved against his touch. And she moved closer until she was practically in his lap. All in all, it was a very good position for her to brush against his erection.

Which is exactly what she did.

She moved. He moved. And, somehow, his erection ended up touching her sex. That created another frenzy of kisses. More movement. More touching.

More of everything.

Oh man, she smelled good. Like sex. She looked even better with her face flushed with arousal and her mouth still damp from their kisses.

More than anything, Logan wanted to finish what he'd started.

He wanted to have sex with her.

But he couldn't.

For one thing, he didn't have a condom. For another, he wasn't sure she was physically ready for sex, since it'd only been six weeks since she'd delivered Tanner.

However, the biggest obstacle was having to live with the consequences of having sex with Mia.

Sex would change things. And she was just starting to trust him. No. He needed to wait until he could assure her safety before he could even think about having a relationship with the mother of his child.

"We're stopping," she said.

"Yeah." Though that one word of agreement hadn't come easily.

His body was still begging and his willpower was zero, but Logan eased her away from him. He went one step further and turned her on her side, so they were in a spooning position. It was far better than the alternative.

No more frontal body contact for them.

Well, not today anyway.

"Say something," she whispered.

"I'm afraid to," Logan admitted.

He held his breath, waiting for her reaction and was surprised when she laughed. It was smoky, thick and laced with arousal. "Have you ever wondered why you're attracted to some people and not others?"

"No. In the past, I've always just gone with it. I'm trying to be more careful with you."

"Careful," she repeated. "That's ironic. Because I've been reckless with you."

He didn't doubt that. Nor did he mind it. Well, his body didn't mind it. His brain was having a little trouble with the fact that he was going to have to be the one to do the resisting.

Logan waited for a lightning bolt to hit him.

Because he knew he stood a snowball's chance in Hades of resisting Mia much longer. He wanted that mouth, that body. Hell, he wanted all of her. Even if wanting her was the last thing he should have on his mind.

Mia turned, rolling on her side so she was

facing him. That wasn't a good move, not with the sexual energy still stirring between them.

"You have something you want to say to me?" she whispered. "Not about the kisses. Or this." She bumped his aroused body with hers and had him seeing stars.

"No. I don't want to talk about that."

But he couldn't help it. He kissed her again. Not a sweet little this-ends-now kiss, either. It was a kiss of hunger. Of frustration. Logan latched on to two handfuls of her hair, dragged her closer and kissed her.

And then, because he knew he had to, he eased her away from him.

"You lost control," she said. "Well, for a few seconds, anyway."

"It won't happen again," he lied.

She stared at him and Logan thought for a moment that she would call his bluff. All it would take was a kiss, a touch or that look in her eyes. But she, too, must have realized the need for some distance because she inched away.

What she didn't do was stop touching him.

She slid her fingers down his chest. "You

want to talk to me about what Jason told you."

Not really—he didn't *want* to have this conversation. But it had to be said because Mia needed to know what he'd learned.

Logan caught her hand to stop the caressing. He was enjoying the heck out of it, but this was info best delivered while in a nonaroused state. "My team found a bug in the diaper bag."

"Donnie Bishop," she immediately offered. She did that caressing thing again. She rubbed her finger along his cheek but then pulled back, knowing it wasn't a good idea. "I should have suspected something when I saw him near the bag at the hospital."

"You had a lot on your mind that night. You'd just witnessed a woman being shot and you'd had bullets fired at you. Anyway, the device is like the one we found on your car. And since you saw him near the diaper bag and since he was on the parking lot surveillance videos, it's a good guess that he's our man. Of course, that doesn't prove he fired shots at us."

"No," she said softly.

Logan hesitated. This wouldn't be as easy to tell her as what she'd already heard.

"Just tell me," Mia insisted. "Even if it's bad, I want to hear it."

"Okay." He nodded. "I have a meeting scheduled with George Devereux tomorrow at the prison. The place is about a half hour outside the city."

"Oh. Well, a meeting with Devereux is a good idea." She didn't sound totally convinced.

"Not really."

She sat partly up, pressed her elbow into the soft mattress and rested her head in her hand. Most of her hesitancy faded. "But it is good. He might be able to tell us who's behind these attempts to kill us. He might even implicate his daughter—"

"He wants you there. In fact, he won't even see me unless I bring you with me."

The hesitancy returned. He felt her body stiffen. "What about Tanner?" she immediately asked.

Logan didn't even have to think about the answer to this. "He's not going to the prison. That's not negotiable. If we make this trip together, then he'll stay with Dorien Novak, the bodyguard that Jason hired." They'd have to time the visit right, of course, so that the baby wouldn't miss being nursed.

But Logan still wasn't convinced this should happen.

"Do you think George Devereux actually has answers for us?"

"Yes," Logan admitted. "But I don't know if he'll actually tell us."

"You think this could be some kind of trick to draw us out into the open?"

"Anything's possible." Logan slid a lock of hair off her cheek.

She stayed quiet a moment. "We don't really have a choice. We'll have to meet with him."

"You have a choice," Logan assured her. "If we don't meet with Devereux, I'll find another way."

"But this is the most readily available way. If he tells us what we need to know so there can be an arrest, then Tanner will be safe."

In theory. Logan knew a million things could go wrong. But things might work out, too, and even though there was only a slim chance of that, it was their best opportunity to identify the person who wanted them dead.

Logan pulled her to him. "You need some sleep. Try to rest."

"You do the same."

He made a sound of agreement, but he knew there was no chance he'd rest.

Because tomorrow morning, the two of them would have to face down a man who might've tried to kill them. Logan prayed that the risk would be worth it and that he could keep Mia and Tanner safe.

Chapter Ten

Mia watched as Logan surrendered his gun to the prison guard.

Just the sight of the high-powered weapon caused her blood pressure to spike, but she was just as scared at the thought of Logan being unarmed. As much as she disliked guns, she equally disliked the fact that he'd just surrendered their main instrument of protection.

They had already been searched, thoroughly. The guards had gone through the pockets and lining of the camel-wool coat that one of Logan's team members had brought over for her earlier that morning. Ditto for her newly acquired chocolate-brown pantsuit. The guards had also searched her purse, though there was little inside it. Her own things—purse and clothes included—were still being examined for bugs and tracking devices.

"It'll be okay," Logan whispered to her. "Is this your first time away from Tanner?"

"Yes." And that was causing her far more concern than she'd imagined it would. It was strange. She'd had a life before Tanner, but everything had changed since his birth. It was getting harder to imagine a time without him.

"We'll keep the meeting short," Logan promised.

He put his hand on the small of her back to lead her through the first set of steel doors. They slid shut behind them and created a sound that made Mia more than a little uncomfortable.

Then there was another security checkpoint, this one with a metal detector that the guard ran over every inch of Logan's body— inside and outside his black leather coat, over his jeans and charcoal-gray shirt. Even his snakeskin boots were checked again. Since they'd both already been searched at the first checkpoint, it seemed a little like overkill, but in this case, Mia knew that it was exactly what was needed.

Logan wouldn't have a weapon.

But then neither would anyone else.

She wanted no repeats of what had happened the day before.

"Inmate Devereux is in here," the guard instructed them, opening the door to a large, austere gray room.

Gray walls, gray floor and dull fluorescent lighting that seemed gray, as well. The only spots of non-gray color were the two black security cameras mounted in the corners.

"Stay on this side of the table," the guard warned. "And don't have any physical contact with the inmate."

"Gladly," Mia mumbled.

She certainly didn't want to get close enough to touch George Devereux. In fact, her goal was to get the information, end this meeting and get back home to her son. She trusted Dorien Novak, but being away from Tanner, especially at a time like this, made her anxiety level skyrocket.

Logan stepped inside the gray room just ahead of her. And he hadn't made it far before he came to an abrupt stop. He cursed, and it was vicious.

Her heart dropped, and she automatically assumed the worst: that Devereux had called off the visit and wasn't there. Or else maybe he was sitting at the table with his own weapon already aimed at them—though that seemed unlikely with an armed guard in the hall and with the surveillance cameras monitoring his every move.

Because Logan was literally blocking her way, Mia had to go on her tiptoes to look over his shoulder to see what had prompted his response.

And she cursed, too.

There was indeed a long metal table, gray, and the man that she presumed was George Devereux was sitting on the far side of it.

But he wasn't alone.

On the near side of the table—the visitors' side—there were already three other people seated.

Royce Foreman, Genevieve Devereux and Donnie Bishop.

What were they doing there? Within just a few yards of her were the four people who might have already tried to kill Logan and her—not once but twice.

It was also likely that those attempts to kill them would continue.

George Devereux certainly wasn't what she'd expected. Despite the prison uniform, he had an air of dignity about him. Along with an expensive haircut and what appeared to be a recent manicure. He'd obviously maintained his well-groomed lifestyle even while behind bars.

Mia disliked him immediately.

"What the hell is going on?" Logan demanded.

"Isn't it obvious—we're about to have a meeting," Devereux answered. He wasn't exactly smiling, but he did seem to be enjoying Logan's displeasure.

But Devereux was the only one of them who was enjoying any of this. The three others were obviously not happy.

Genevieve had her shapely legs crossed, her arms folded over her ample chest and her red stiletto-clad right foot was swinging furiously at the empty space between her and the table. She wasn't looking at her father.

Nor was Royce, who was staring at the wall. He seemed more disinterested than annoyed.

And then there was Donnie Bishop.

No purple jacket today. He wore rumpled jeans and an equally rumpled college sweat-shirt. And unlike their other encounter, he wasn't smirking. His mouth was tight and he was stewing.

Mia felt both curious and concerned about what was about to happen.

The entire room felt ready to explode.

"George ordered us to come," Donnie an-nounced. "He said there'd be hell to pay if I didn't get my butt here at this ungodly hour of the morning."

"I merely wanted to get a few things straight and needed you all here to do that," Devereux insisted, turning his cool green eyes on Donnie. "An ungodly hour or so of your time isn't much, considering."

Devereux turned his attention to Logan. "I understand you've been making accusations about my daughter."

"Logan thinks I tricked that woman into being my surrogate," Genevieve added without looking at either of them. Her foot worked even faster and the grip she had on her own arms was so tight that Mia suspected she'd have bruises. "He thinks I wanted to trap him by having someone else give birth to his child."

"I haven't made any false accusations," Logan said. "Everything I've said about Genevieve is true."

"Ha!" laughed Genevieve. "You wouldn't know the truth if it hit you in the face. I don't deserve this, Logan." She swirled around in her seat, but the moment her eyes landed on him, her expression softened a bit. And then it softened a lot. "Can't we just sit down together, alone, and talk this out?"

"I don't think that'd be a good idea," Royce insisted. He sounded both jealous and concerned for safety.

Logan shook his head. "Anything you want to say to me, you can say here."

"In front of her?" Genevieve stabbed her index finger at Mia. "Hardly. She's to blame for this. We could have worked things out if she hadn't come to you with these ridiculous lies."

Genevieve's resentment didn't surprise Mia, but it did surprise her that the woman believed that she could actually work things out with Logan. Genevieve was clearly delusional. Unfortunately, someone who was delusional could do all sorts of nasty things, including but not limited to attempted murder.

Scowling, Donnie stood and outstretched his arms, palms up. "This is why I'm frickin' here—to rehash an old lovers' quarrel?"

"You're here because you're a suspect," Devereux calmly clarified. He motioned for Donnie to sit. "You had the means, motive and opportunity for the shooting incident that left Collena Drake wounded. A shooting incident that could have harmed Logan and Ms. Crandall."

"I can be a suspect without having to be subjected to this conversation," Donnie fired back. "The soaps start in an hour and I don't intend to miss them."

"I've never asked you for a favor," Devereux continued. "Considering I've made you lots of money—"

"And you've gotten me into a whole

yacht-load of trouble with your investment recommendations."

"Yes. But you're still rich and, unlike me, you're not in jail. So, consider that favor and think about the consequences of refusing me this favor."

That stopped Donnie in his tracks. He huffed and turned back around. "And what favor would that be?"

"Convince Logan to stop this witch-hunt investigation against Genevieve."

"Witch hunt?" Donnie repeated. "Is that what you call it these days?"

Devereux nodded. "There is no evidence to prove otherwise, *is there?*"

Mia didn't think that was an off-the-cuff comment. Was Devereux referring to the incriminating recordings that Donnie supposedly had? Or did he even know about them? Considering everything she'd heard about Devereux, he *likely* knew. And if so, was that some kind of veiled threat for Donnie to keep quiet?

Donnie certainly didn't acknowledge it. He turned to walk away again but stopped when he was side-by-side with Logan and

Mia. He put his arms around each of them and brought them into a huddle. "When you're done with this trivial stuff, meet me in the parking lot. I'll give you a sample of what we discussed earlier."

A sample of the recordings that would hopefully implicate Genevieve. Donnie apparently had decided to put his trust in Logan rather than George Devereux.

Of course, it was bold—and even stupid—to make an offer like that in a room where Devereux could easily overhear it. Mia didn't like the tangled, dangerous turn this conversation was taking.

Logan didn't say anything until Donnie had left. "Let's cut to the chase. I need someone here to admit guilt—either their own or someone else's. Because I want these attacks on Mia and my son to stop."

Genevieve gave Logan an icy glare when he said *my son.* "The guilty party just walked out of the room," she insisted. "Or else she's standing right by you."

Logan looked at Royce. "I'm not sure about that."

"Neither am I," Devereux volunteered.

"Genevieve, Royce, why don't you two step outside for a moment while I have a chat with Logan and his lady?"

Genevieve mumbled a protest under her breath. Royce made a sound of annoyance, but they both stood.

"Tell the guard that I'll be ready to return to my cell in ten minutes," Devereux instructed his daughter.

That request caused her to grumble even more. Genevieve walked toward the door, but then stopped when she reached Logan. She was so close that Mia could smell the woman's expensive perfume.

"You have this all wrong," Genevieve whispered to Logan. "I would never do anything to hurt you. In your heart, you must know that."

"I know no such thing."

Much to Mia's surprise, tears sprang to Genevieve's eyes and they looked real. She quickly wiped away those tears and both Royce and she did as her father had asked. They left the room and shut the door behind them.

"So far, you've wasted my time," Logan immediately told Devereux.

"Yes. I'm sorry about that. I really thought having everyone in the room would be more beneficial to the truth coming out. But not to worry. I have something that should make this visit worthwhile. I did some checking. That woman you rescued in South America had some local enemies. And one enemy in particular might be responsible for the shooting and the explosion."

Logan shrugged. "So I've heard."

Well, Mia certainly hadn't heard about it. She pulled in her breath and looked at Logan. "What is he talking about?"

"I was going to tell you," Logan assured her.

But he didn't get a chance to do that because Devereux continued, seemingly pleased that this was the first Mia was hearing about the connection between Logan's work and the recent attacks.

"Then you probably know that Royce was one of the woman's enemies," Devereux announced. He stared at Mia. "It was business, but sometimes Royce takes business personally. Royce wanted something that the woman had and when she was kidnapped, he thought he would get it. Logan ruined everything for him by rescuing the woman in what was considered by most to be an unrecoverable situation."

And that rescue was related to Royce. More puzzle pieces. But how did they fit?

"Is this leading somewhere?" Logan asked impatiently.

"It is. Royce has a strong motive for wanting you dead. He wants revenge."

So, that's how the pieces fit. "Does that motive extend to me and my son?" Mia asked.

Devereux hesitated a moment. "It could. Royce might feel the best way to get back at Logan is to hurt those close to him. He admitted to me that he'd kept an eye on Logan after he got back from South America. Royce could have learned that you'd given birth to Logan's child."

Logan latched on to that. "Other than through Genevieve, how would Royce have learned about my son?"

"The same way you did, I suspect. Probably by following you and then piecing together the same clues you did."

Well, maybe those pieces fit or maybe Devereux was giving them this information for a different reason. "And your pointing the finger at Royce might be a way of trying to take the guilt off Genevieve."

The man nodded. "It's true. I'd prefer you go after Royce."

"I'm going after whoever's guilty."

"Admirable."

"You should try it sometime." Logan propped his hands on his hips. "So, if you think Royce is the culprit, why did you invite Donnie Bishop to this meeting?"

"Ah. Well, that was for my own information. I wanted to see how he would react to certain comments. I think he might be the one who's trying to set up Genevieve. Yes, it's true that she wanted to have your baby, but she didn't go through with the surrogacy plan."

Logan groaned. "Your daughter is more than capable of putting together a plan like this. Why can't you see that?"

"I do see it," Devereux admitted. He looked at Mia. "But now that you have a child, certainly you can put yourself in my shoes. Imagine that it's your son who's being accused of a heinous crime that could land him in jail. Wouldn't you do anything to make sure that didn't happen?"

"No. There are no excuses for criminal behavior."

Devereux shrugged. "Then we agree to disagree."

"Not quite," Logan insisted. "Who's trying to kill us? And don't guess—I want the truth."

"I don't know the truth, but if I had to put money on someone, it'd be Royce. You already know that I don't believe my daughter could do something like that. And Donnie, well, Donnie is self-centered and ambitious, but he doesn't have a knack for violence. I don't doubt his involvement with the surrogacy plan, but if he had anything to do with the shooting, then he hired someone to do his dirty work."

"Genevieve could have done the same."

Another shrug, and Devereux dismissed it with the flick of his hand. "Someone is digging through Royce's background. Specifically, they're trying to learn if he's had any experience with explosives. I assume the person digging works for you." He didn't wait for Logan to confirm or deny that. "Royce has that kind of experience. He had a brief relationship in college with a young woman whose brother was a demolitions expert. According to my sources, the brother taught Royce some things."

So, Royce had the expertise to blow things up. But the real question was: had he?

"Another thing," Devereux went on. "Whatever Donnie tells you about Genevieve, don't believe it. He'll do anything to make sure he doesn't go to jail for what happened at Brighton."

"Old news from an old, unreliable source. Is that it?" Logan asked.

"Not quite. One last word of warning. Collena Drake."

Logan just stared about him. "What about her?"

"She might have other motives that you're not privy to. We do know that she was involved at Brighton as well."

"She was an undercover cop," Logan fired back. "And she's innocent. Remember, she got shot while trying to give us information."

"Shot but not killed or even hurt that seriously. She could have orchestrated it herself."

"And why the hell would she have done that?" Logan asked, though he probably figured all of this was Devereux's smokescreen to take the blame off Genevieve.

Well, it wasn't working.

"People have all sorts of reasons for doing things," Devereux concluded. "Collena Drake is no different."

Logan dismissed that with a shake of his head, and he caught Mia's arm as they left the room. Mia had plenty of questions about the meeting, but she figured they'd have to wait because she expected to run into Royce and Genevieve.

But they weren't there.

"The others already left," the guard informed them. "Said they'd be back later."

"They left together with the other man, Donnie Bishop?" Logan asked.

The guard shook his head. "All three left alone. Ms. Devereux was the last to leave."

He led them down the corridor and toward the security checkpoints.

Logan didn't say anything because he didn't want anyone, including the guards, to hear their conversation about Devereux. They collected their coats and his weapon as they proceeded through the checkpoints and returned to the main entrance of the prison.

"I didn't tell you about Royce's connection to the woman I rescued in South America because I was waiting on the report from my team. Obviously Devereux moved a little faster than my team did."

"Or maybe he already knew the information," Mia pointed out. "Considering how protective he is of his daughter, he probably would have had Royce investigated."

"True."

Mia buttoned her coat before they stepped outside. But even with the coat and the wool-blend pants and jacket, the cold air rifled right through her. "So, what was that about Collena Drake? You don't think she could have anything to do with this?"

"No. I had her thoroughly investigated. She was pregnant when she heard about the illegal activity going on at Brighton, and she went undercover for weeks to try to figure out what was going on. The clinic director found out what Collena was doing and gave her a drug to induce labor. Once she delivered the baby, someone stole her newborn and tried to kill her."

Mia felt instant empathy with the woman. Mercy, what they'd both been through as a result of their association with Brighton. "Then why did Devereux warn us about her? And for that matter, what was this meeting all about?"

Logan must have noticed that she was cold because he slipped his arm around her. "Well, for one thing he apparently wanted to threaten Donnie to prevent him from giving us any information about Genevieve."

She agreed with that. "And he also wanted to make us think that Royce was guilty. Anything other than blame his daughter. Would he kill to save Genevieve?" Mia asked.

"In a heartbeat."

Mia was afraid of that.

They stopped just outside the massive

twelve-foot-high front entry gates and looked around the parking lot.

There was no sign of Royce or Genevieve.

And there was no sign of Donnie, either.

Logan turned, glancing at the dozens of cars that lined the parking lot. "I guess Donnie decided not to wait around for us, after all."

Great. And here Mia thought at least something good would come from this. Without Donnie's sample recordings, this meeting had been a total waste of time.

"Why would Donnie tell us to meet him out here if he had no plans to stay?" Mia asked, checking her watch. It was still well over two hours to Tanner's next feeding, but she didn't want to spend time waiting around the prison.

"Maybe Devereux's subtle threats got to Donnie and he changed his mind." Logan glanced around them. "Let's go. Once we're in the car, I'll call him and see what the heck is going on."

Logan hadn't parked far from the entrance. In fact, just the second row over, but the brutal wind would make the short walk seem much longer.

"Wait," she heard Logan say.

Mia turned her head to glance at him, to see what had prompted him to say that. But out of the corner of her eye, she saw Logan move. Fast.

He plowed into her and shoved her to the cement.

Mia landed hard, her hands and knees catching the brunt of her fall. Her brain didn't even have time to register the pain when she heard the blast.

"Stay down," Logan warned. "Someone just took a shot at us."

Chapter Eleven

Logan scrambled to cover Mia's body with his own.

He prayed it wasn't too late.

He couldn't see where the shot had landed, but it couldn't have been far. And that meant the shooter probably wasn't too far away.

Hell.

Judging from the sound of the shot, it'd come from some kind of assault rifle.

Who would be so bold, so desperate or just so plain stupid to fire shots in front of a prison?

Unfortunately, any of their suspects might be responsible, but he couldn't worry about that now. Right now, he had to keep Mia from being hurt.

There was another shot. This one zinged into the concrete right next to them and kicked up chunks of debris and dust. Logan knew he couldn't stay put. He needed to take cover behind one of the cars because those flying bits of concrete could be just as dangerous as a bullet.

Another bullet came at them.

He tracked the sound and thought it might be coming from across the road where there was a cluster of thick trees. Someone could easily hide there. It was a high ground. Perfect position for an ambush.

The next shot smacked into the high metal fence and set off alarms.

"Thank God," Logan mumbled. Maybe now the guards would come running to investigate because he was in desperate need of some backup.

But guards and backup wouldn't solve his immediate problem. Another bullet came at them. Then another, until the shots were nonstop. A barrage of deadly gunfire and each bullet could be lethal.

"We have to move," he told Mia.

Since there was no break in the shots, he knew he had to pray for the best and go for it. Logan lifted his gun and fired into the cluster of trees. Of course, he was way out of range with his handgun, but he hoped it would buy them a little time.

He fired again and caught her arm. "Let's go," Logan insisted.

Logan didn't waste any time. Nor did he let her get to a standing position where she'd be too easy a target. Instead, he crouched in front of her and practically dragged her toward a dark-blue SUV.

He pushed her down on the concrete sidewalk just in front of the vehicle and, as he'd done before, used his body to shelter her. The position put a lot of pressure on his right leg and almost immediately the pain began to stab through him. Logan pushed that pain aside so he could assess their situation and get them the heck out of there.

The SUV was large enough to give them some protection, but the gunman obviously tracked them to their new position because the next bullet ripped through the passenger door of the SUV.

Behind him, he heard a much more welcome sound. The shouts of a guard. At least one. Maybe more.

"Stay down," he repeated to Mia when she tried to lift her head to see what the heck was going on.

Logan wanted to know that himself.

"Over here," he shouted to the guards so they wouldn't mistake him for the gunman. The last thing he needed was for anyone else to start firing at them. "I think the shooter's in the trees across the road."

A bulky uniformed guard took up position at the main gate and, using a concrete pylon for cover, returned fire.

So did the shooter.

However, he or she didn't aim for the guard. The person continued to shoot at Mia and Logan.

Beside him, Logan could hear Mia's rough, jagged breath. He glanced at her to make sure she was okay. She was pale and trembling but, other than that, was holding up well. Far better than he'd expected. That was a miracle, considering his gun was in plain sight and someone was trying to kill them—again.

As the bullets continued to pelt the SUV and the prison fence, anger began to boil inside Logan. He was sick of this. He'd chosen a dangerous career and life, but Mia had done all she could to avoid it. Yet, here she was, tossed into a firestorm not of her own making. She was a victim again and that riled him to the core. How dare this shooting SOB put her through this?

The only saving grace was that this time, Tanner wasn't with them. He was safe back at the hotel with the bodyguard. Soon, Logan would have Mia back there as well, but first he had to get past this gunman.

The shots stopped.

Just like that. There were no more thick blasts, only the howl of the winter wind and the sound of Logan's heartbeat pounding in his ears.

"Who's out there shooting?" the guard shouted to Logan. Another armed guard took position behind the pylon opposite his comrade.

"I don't know," Logan shouted back. "But I intend to find out."

Another pair of guards raced toward the gate, both of them with two-handed grips on their semiautomatic weapons. But neither of them could come out into the parking lot because the shots started up again. The rifleman had obviously reloaded.

How long was this going to go on?

Each second, each shot, was like an eternity.

Even though Mia and he were partly protected by the SUV, Logan knew that each new round fired could be potentially fatal. Bullets could ricochet, eat their way through metal and glass.

He needed to get closer to those trees so he could get a better shot. He probably couldn't get within range of the shooter, but maybe, just maybe, he could get close enough to get the idiot to stop.

"Wait here," Logan told Mia.

There was another advantage to his trying to get closer to the shooter. If he moved, he could probably draw the fire away from Mia and get a better angle to see—and stop— whoever was out there.

Mia caught his arm and frantically shook her head. "What are you going to do?"

"You'll be safe. Just stay down. No matter what. *Stay down.*"

"Please don't go."

He wasn't immune to the fear he heard in her voice. Or was that concern he heard? Logan thought she might be angry at his plan of action, but he didn't have time to explain what he needed to do. "I have to do this."

She was still shaking her head when he moved away from her. He stayed in a crouched position and tried to use the other vehicles as cover while he made his way laterally across the parking lot.

The first part of his plan worked.

The shooter fired at him.

His leg throbbed, protesting the strain that he was putting on his still-healing muscles, but Logan kept moving. And he kept watching to make sure Mia stayed put and for any sign of the shooter in those trees.

Unfortunately, thick gray clouds had covered most of the sky so there was no sunlight to catch even a glint of gunmetal.

He ducked in front of a red two-door car. A split-second later, a bullet shattered the windshield. Logan was thankful for each miss, but he knew he couldn't assume that the gunman was a bad shot. Of course, that *was* a possibility—and if so, he was dealing with an amateur.

Which meant the gunman could be Donnie Bishop, Genevieve or Royce.

Or it could be a pro who was just having a bad day.

Logan glanced at Mia. She was still crouched in front of the SUV and she was staring at him. The prison guards were still in place, and one of them was talking on a two-way radio. Logan figured it wouldn't be long before police backup arrived. After all, this wasn't a prison incident and the local authorities would no doubt be called in.

Maybe the authorities would get lucky and catch the SOB.

But just in case they didn't arrive in time, Logan raced toward another vehicle. The shooter followed him with another round of shots. However, the new position was worth it. It put him at the far end of the parking lot, where there were fewer obstructions.

And he finally saw the shooter.

Like the other attack in front of Mia's house, Logan couldn't tell if the shooter was male or female. The person wore black bulky clothes and was literally perched in a tree about five hundred yards on the other side of the road. Well out of range of Logan's Glock.

He inched forward, staying next to the vehicle, but this was no longer a lateral reposition. Logan was moving toward the shooter and would continue to so long as the person took aim at him and not Mia.

Plus, by getting closer, Logan might be able to get off his own shot, and he could perhaps figure out who was under all that bulky black clothing.

When he reached the end of the car, he raced toward the second row of vehicles. Logan heard the sirens then and knew the authorities were on the way. He also heard something else.

The sound of the next shot.

This one didn't come toward him. It had been fired in Mia's direction.

"Hell," he snarled. That did it. Logan was well past his boiling point and he came up ready to blast that moron to smithereens.

Logan fired.

Keeping track of his own shots. He had

thirteen rounds and had already used two. He clipped off two more, and he knew that while he didn't have the range, he damn sure had the accuracy. His bullets went right at the shooter.

"Logan, get down!" he heard Mia yell.

But he didn't, even though it was a risk. There was a chance that he could end this right here, right now.

Evidently, the gunman thought that, as well.

Because the person stopped firing and began to scramble down the tree. That was Logan's cue to move—fast.

Logan stopped inching forward and broke into a run. He had to hurdle over fallen trees and underbrush. That didn't help the pain in his leg, but he refused to let it stop him. He ran as hard as he could, trying to make up the distance between the shooter and him.

He lost sight of the person just as he reached the edge of the road. Going into the thick woods wasn't his first choice of things to do, but he figured the gunman was well on his way to escaping.

He wasn't going to let that happen.

Because if he or she got away, there'd only be another attack. And another. Until Logan put a stop to this.

The sirens grew closer, but Logan didn't wait for them since they were probably still a minute or more out. The shooter would be long gone by then.

He hurried across the road and ducked behind a tree. Logan did a quick visual check around him and raced forward to the spot where he'd first seen the gunman.

The person wasn't there, of course.

But there were some spent shell casings and trampled leaves that left a clear trail to the shooter's exit path.

Logan followed with his gun aimed and ready.

He moved through the maze of trees and prickly shrubs, and he listened for any sound to indicate that the shooter had doubled back and was about to ambush him.

But that wasn't the sound he heard.

Even over the shrill of the approaching sirens, he heard something he didn't want to hear.

The sound of someone starting a car engine.

He cursed and continued to race through the woods. He pinpointed his focus on the sound of that car and tried to shut out everything else. This was his chance to make sure Mia and his son were safe.

Maybe his only chance.

Logan slapped aside a low-hanging tree branch and saw the clearing. He raced toward it. But it wasn't just a clearing. It was a narrow country road, and there was a dark-green car parked next to a shallow ditch.

The person dressed in black bulky clothing was in that car.

Logan could see the shadowy figure through the heavily tinted windows, but he couldn't make out any distinguishing features.

But that was the least of his problems.

The driver hit the accelerator.

Logan tried to stop the escape. He ran toward the road, aimed his weapon and fired. His bullet shattered the glass in the back window.

But the driver didn't stop.

He fired again, but he took his focus off the driver and turned it to the license plates.

VMJ were the first three letters. He didn't get a good look at the rest because the car barreled over a hill.

And disappeared.

With his breath gusting and adrenaline firing on all cylinders, he repeated those three letters, committing them to memory.

Because those three letters were going to lead him to the person who'd just tried to murder them once again.

Chapter Twelve

The hot bath hadn't helped Mia.

Neither had the chamomile tea that Logan had delivered to the suite. Ditto for the chicken soup she'd had for dinner. Even holding, nursing and rocking Tanner hadn't worked. Instead of spending pleasant quiet moments with her son, her mind and heart were still racing with the most unpleasant thing of all.

She couldn't stop thinking about the shooting.

They had come close to dying again. Another attack, another near miss. And they still didn't have a culprit identified and behind bars.

However, Mia refused to give in to the helpless feeling that their situation was creating. She refused to cry and she darn sure refused to give up. The stakes were too high for her to do that. Besides, Logan was working on the case. She had to believe that sooner or later—hopefully sooner—he'd be able to put a name and a face with the person who had fired rifle shots at them.

She eased Tanner into his bassinet and went to the door that separated the bedroom from the sitting area. Logan was still on the phone. He had the call on speakerphone and she could hear bits and pieces of what he and Jason were saying. However, Logan's tone told her a lot more than his words.

He was barking out orders, which meant he was still well beyond being riled.

That didn't surprise her. He'd been in that particular state of mind since he'd stormed out of those woods near the prison. Mia had been so thankful to see him, so thankful that he was alive and unharmed. But Logan had immediately launched into an investigation that included phoning for members of his team to find the car that the gunman had used to escape.

Logan had wanted to go after the car himself.

He'd as much as said so when they were giving their statements to Sheriff Knight, the officer who'd responded to the scene. The sheriff, however, had advised Logan to take Mia and go someplace safe, since the shooter might return for another round.

Mia tiptoed into the sitting room so that she wouldn't disturb his call. They were alone. Dorien Novak, the bodyguard, had excused herself to go to her room across the hall. Mia figured the woman really just wanted to get away from a snarling, scowling Logan.

And speaking of Logan, he was indeed still scowling as he listened to Jason explain some paperwork. Logan was sitting on the sofa, his feet propped on the ottoman. He'd taken off his boots and jacket and had discarded them on the floor next to his suitcase. His shirt was halfway unbuttoned, revealing a tightly muscled chest sprinkled with dark coils of hair.

Despite the nightmare they'd just been through, or maybe as a result of it, she felt herself go all warm.

Okay, hot.

It was strange, the effect he had on her. Even now, she could appreciate and react to the sight of him.

She stepped closer and spotted the uneaten sandwich and coffee on the table next to the baby monitor equipped with a camera. And his gun, which he'd covered with a cloth napkin. He hadn't touched either the sandwich or the coffee, though it was nearly six in the evening, which meant he'd skipped both lunch and dinner. He had to be starving by now.

Logan looked at her, snared her gaze. And he seemed to do a double take. The look he gave her was long. Smoldering.

And if she wasn't mistaken—appreciative.

Mia immediately glanced down to make sure she hadn't left her top unbuttoned after nursing, but she was thankfully covered.

Well, almost.

She'd changed since the incident at the prison and was wearing one of the outfits Logan's team had sent to the hotel. It definitely wasn't her normal attire. A short black skirt and a loose citrus-green shirt that barely made it to her waist.

Logan returned his attention to the phone when Jason finished speaking. "Please tell me that the car dealer had surveillance videos on the lot or in his office," he said to the man.

"Afraid not. It's a mom-and-pop place out past Kerrville. They probably only sell a handful of cars each month, if that."

Despite that dour-sounding news, it was also promising because it sounded as if they'd found the place where the gunman had bought the escape vehicle.

"Besides," Jason continued. "The dealer is pretty sure the guy who bought it wasn't buying it for himself. He claimed that his name was David Smith and he paid cash."

"So the person could have been buying the car for Genevieve," Logan concluded.

"Unfortunately, yes."

That was unfortunate. Because if the shooter had used a go-between for the sale, then his or her identity was still a secret.

"Call me the minute you have an update on Collena or anything else," Logan insisted. He stabbed the end call button and angled his body so that he was facing her. "How's Tanner?"

"Asleep."

He made a rumbling sound deep within his throat and rubbed his hands over his face. "I'm glad he's too young to know what's going on."

Mia walked closer and sank down on the ottoman across from him. "What exactly is going on? Did Jason have any news?"

"Nothing that pleases me."

He turned again on the sofa, the movement dragging the right side of his shirt wider open so that it exposed even more of his chest. She'd been right about the tight muscles, but she also saw the scars. One angled across his left pec, and because his jeans rode loose and low on his hips, she could also see another one on his equally tightly muscled abdomen.

"How did that happen?" Without thinking, Mia reached out and traced her finger over the scar on his abdomen.

She knew it was a mistake when she heard Logan draw in his breath. It wasn't an ordinary breath. Nor was it sharp or even the sound of surprise. It was a low husky male sound that stirred the heat inside her again. The sound a man would make when having great sex.

That had her drawing her hand back. "Sorry." She shook her head and silently cursed. What was wrong with her? "Uh, you were talking about Jason."

Logan waited a moment, staring at her. "Jason traced the license plates to a dealership. Someone bought the vehicle yesterday afternoon, but you heard that it's a dead end."

"Maybe not." She took a deep breath to try to keep her head clear. "Maybe once the vehicle is found—"

"My team found it about a half hour ago. It was in the parking lot of an abandoned warehouse in south San Antonio. Someone had set fire to it and there doesn't appear to be any recoverable evidence."

After hearing that, it was difficult not to give in to the disappointment, but Mia knew that Logan didn't need any more frustration.

He was feeling enough for both of them.

"What about Collena?" she asked. "How is she?"

Logan shook his head. "Good news on that front. She's better. She's supposed to meet with her doctor this afternoon and I'm getting an update once she's spoken to him. If she's going home anytime soon, I need to arrange security to monitor her house because I can't rule out that she's still a target, too."

In fact, there wasn't much of anything they could rule out. They still had four suspects: George Devereux, Genevieve, Royce and Donnie. And any one of them could have fired the shots or hired someone to do the job.

"You have so much on your mind," she mumbled.

"What about you?" His eyes skimmed over her again. From head to toe. "How are you doing?"

He reached out and caught her hand. Mia tried not to wince, but his touch, no matter how slight, caused the scrapes on her palms to sting. The scrapes she'd gotten when he'd pushed her to the ground in the parking lot.

Still, she preferred having his touch. For some reason, in addition to making her hotter than summer asphalt, Logan made her feel safe.

But she rethought that.

He didn't just make her feel safe—he made her *feel*. And that in itself was nothing short of a miracle. He'd accomplished what years of therapy couldn't.

"I'm doing a lot better than you think I am." She forced herself to smile. "Logan, what happened at the prison wasn't your fault."

"Like hell it wasn't."

Just like that, the tender moment was over. He got up, shoved his cell phone into the pocket of his jeans and walked to the bar.

Or rather, he limped to the bar.

He poured himself a glass of the Kentucky bourbon he'd had delivered to the room and he took the shot in one gulp. It must have been strong because it watered his eyes.

Mia got up and went to him. "We went there looking for information. Now, whether it was a setup or not, it still wasn't your fault. We can't stop looking for the truth and stayed cocooned in here."

"I can keep you cocooned." And he looked her straight in the eyes when he said that. "I can't put you in harm's way anymore."

"That's not really your decision to make, is it?" Mia pointed out.

Anger flared through him. "You bet it is. I got you into this mess—"

"I got *you* into this mess," Mia countered. But then she shook her head. "This discussion is obviously not going anywhere. We should be putting the blame on the shooter and not ourselves." She glanced down at his leg. "You're in pain."

At first, he looked as if he were about to deny it. "Some," he finally said.

She stepped closer and slid her arm around his waist. For her, it was a bold move. After all, they were alone and the energy between them was intense.

"A hot bath might help, or so I heard someone say," she said, trying to keep her tone soothing. Unfortunately, it came out as sultry. She heard her own low silky voice and fought the urge to run her fingers over his stomach again.

He lifted an eyebrow. "Is that an invitation?"

She smiled again, but it faded as quickly as it came. That's because she had to wonder—was it really an honest-to-goodness invitation or just the adrenaline talking? After all, she was standing very close to the hottest man she'd ever known. A man she desperately wanted.

But was afraid to take.

So had the bath been her wussy way of offering herself to Logan? Mia wasn't sure, but she figured there was an easy way to find out. She reached up to touch his face. However, reaching was as far as she got.

Logan snagged her wrist and examined the scrapes on her right hand. Then he cursed.

Oh, mercy. She hadn't intended for him to see that.

"It looks worse than it is," she said, trying to soothe some of that reborn anger.

"I did that."

"Yes, when you saved my life. Or maybe it happened when you put your body over mine so that you'd get shot and I wouldn't. Either way, I owe you and these scrapes are a minor price to pay for being alive."

Logan obviously didn't agree because he cursed again and would have moved away from her if she hadn't latched on to his arm.

Mia didn't allow doubts to enter her head. She leaned in to kiss him.

But he beat her to it.

His mouth came to hers. The kiss was hard and hungry and Mia knew this wasn't going to stop. She didn't want it to stop. And the kiss wasn't all she wanted to do. No. She fulfilled a little fantasy and ran her uninjured left hand down the length of his chest. Oh, yes. It was a great chest. And an even better stomach. Lot of muscles. Lots of strength. His reaction was good, too.

He caught her wrist and slid her hand lower, over the front of his jeans.

Logan made that male sound again. The one that melted her body and made her want more.

So she took more.

She shook off his grip and slid her hand inside his jeans. If she thought her pulse was jumping and body burning before that, it was a mild reaction compared to having him hard and ready in the palm of her hand.

Logan pulled back from the kiss and looked at her. He seemed to be examining her eyes, maybe to figure out if this was going where he thought it was. But while he watched her, while those sizzling eyes met hers, he took his own hand up her right thigh. He didn't move fast, at least not fast enough for her now-burning body. He gave her enough time to stop it.

But she had no intentions of stopping anything.

"I haven't had an orgasm in three years," she admitted.

That information caused a muscle to flicker in his jaw. "Then you're overdue for at least a couple."

While he tongue-kissed her neck and earlobe, Logan pushed up her skirt and his hand slid to her stomach. Then, lower.

Into her panties.

He didn't just touch her with his fingers. He went inside her. Touching her in just the right place.

Just like that, the sensations wracked her. The fire blazed through her. The need pinpointed to his touch.

Her climax came in a flash. So fast. So hard. So intense. So overwhelming that she would have fallen if he hadn't caught her. Her body closed around his fingers. And Mia felt herself fly right over the edge.

"That's one," Logan said.

Right before he dragged her to the floor.

Chapter Thirteen

Logan refused to think about this.

And he wouldn't consider stopping.

That probably had something to do with the fact that Mia had her hand in his jeans. Her fingers were wrapped around him.

Or maybe it was because of the sweet silky moans she was making as she felt the aftershocks of her orgasm. It didn't matter why he was doing this or why he wasn't stopping. Hell, it didn't even matter if this was wrong. They were well past the point of logic, of doing the right thing.

Taking Mia was the only thing that mattered.

They landed on the soft carpeted floor, side by side. Face-to-face. Thankfully, other parts of them were aligned, as well.

If her injured hand bothered her, she certainly didn't show any signs of it. His leg was hurting, he was sure of it, but the pain was numbed from his overwhelming need to take Mia *now*.

Because her fingers began to slide up and down the length of him, Logan took her hand from his jeans.

Mia slid down, her mouth against his chest. And she kissed him, using her tongue and mouth to turn up the heat a notch. Not that he needed those kisses—he was primed—but he took a moment to savor what would likely be very short foreplay.

He'd thought the first climax would take the edge off for her. But it apparently had only made her want him more. Her kisses were urgent, almost frantic. And she didn't keep her hands still, either. She slid them over him as if she knew the very secrets of what got him hot.

And she probably did.

Since his body was craving any and everything she wanted to do to him.

Because he wanted to give her more pleasure, Logan turned the tables on her. He slid down her body and stripped off her top so she could deliver some tongue kisses of his own. He kissed the tops of her breasts and had the pleasure of hearing that silky moan. He made her moan even harder when he took those kisses lower.

Man, she smelled like sex. And he wanted nothing more than to have that taste in his mouth. So, that's what he did. Logan rid her of her panties and gave her some kisses that she would hopefully never forget.

He certainly wouldn't.

She tasted as good as she smelled. Her cries roared through him, fueling the need that was already overwhelming.

Mia rammed her fingers through his hair. "Again," she whispered.

Oh, yeah. He intended to do that, too, but this time, he wanted to be inside her.

Logan left her for a couple of seconds so he could fumble through his leather bag and find the condoms he'd had brought from his house. Mia followed him. That was a sight, all right. A beautifully naked Mia crawling her way toward him.

With those jeweled amber eyes and her coppery hair spilling all around her face, she was a vision. Apparently, a needy one, because she practically tackled him.

He landed on his back, with her on top of him. All in all, it was a good position.

Until he remember something.

"Are you physically ready for this?" he asked, dreading that she might say no.

"I'm more than ready," she assured him. And she proved it by unzipping his jeans and stripping them off him.

Yes, she was ready. Mentally. But Logan forced himself to slow down just in case her body wasn't on the same willing level as the rest of her.

She helped him with the condom and damn near gave him a climax in the process. Logan rolled them over, so that he was on top of her. And because he couldn't wait any longer, he entered her. Gently.

He felt her body give way to him as he pushed through that silky heat. The pleasure was so intense that Logan lost his breath and didn't care if he ever found it.

And then Mia froze.

Startled, his gaze flew to hers. Her face was still flushed with arousal, and the heat was still in her eyes. "I'm claustrophobic," she said. "I've never had sex with a man on top of me."

Logan immediately started to change their positions so that she could be on top. But she latched on to him with both hands and even wrapped her legs around him.

"No, this is fine." The words spilled out, mixed with her rapid raw breath. "Better than fine. This is the way I want it, Logan. This is the way I want you."

She lifted her hips, pushing him deeper inside her.

That did it. Logan took her assurance at face value and went with it. Later, much later, he'd consider what a gift of trust this was from her. But right now, he wanted a different kind of gift. One that would satisfy the heat raging inside.

He moved inside her. Long, penetrating strokes. Strokes that she deepened even more by moving with him. Each one took them closer. Higher. To the only place that either of them wanted to go.

"Again," Mia whispered, the sound shuddering on her lips.

Logan obliged.

He slid into her one last time. He felt her body respond in the most basic, human way.

Her fingers dug into his back. Her legs clamped harder around him. And Logan kissed her so he could taste her as she shattered again.

THE SOUND WOKE HIM UP.

Logan snapped to a sitting position and reached for his gun. That was there. He fumbled around. Still didn't find it. And the sound continued.

It took him a moment to orient himself. He glanced at the clock that was perched on a nightstand. According to the ruby-red numerals it was nearly 9:00 p.m. Thankfully, there was light spilling from the adjoining bathroom so he could see where he was.

He was in the hotel bed with Mia.

She stirred, too, though she didn't immediately sit up. "Tanner," she mumbled.

That was the sound Logan had heard. Not an intruder or a gunman. His son was awake and was fussing, probably because he needed to be changed or fed.

Mia yawned and shoved her hair from her face. She looked disoriented, as well. And totally hot. Just the sight of her naked body made Logan want her all over again, but that would have to wait. Tanner got priority.

"How did we get in bed?" she asked, yawning again. She fumbled around the nightstand, located a nightgown and pulled it on.

"I moved you here after you fell asleep on the floor. You were obviously exhausted."

And she was also a little disoriented because she didn't get up. Logan climbed from the bed, put on his boxers and went to the bassinet to get Tanner. He scooped him up in his arms and brought him to Mia.

Though she was obviously still tired, Mia took over. She pushed aside one side of her gown and Tanner latched on to her nipple so he could nurse.

That was a sight, too, and it elicited a totally different response in Logan. Mia with their child in her arms. It made him feel warm and fuzzy.

It also made him even more concerned.

So far, he'd done a lousy job protecting them. Having sex with Mia amid all the danger was definitely a lapse in judgment and concentration. Protecting them should be his only focus.

"I've never had sex on the floor before," she mumbled, her eyes meeting his. "It was great." But then Mia frowned. "I know it also complicates things."

Logan didn't dare say he was thinking the same thing. He just let her continue.

"You can interpret it whatever way you like," she said.

He flexed his eyebrows. It couldn't happen again. At least not until they'd caught the person who was trying to kill them.

The silence settled uncomfortably between them. The only sound was of Tanner nursing and that wasn't enough to block out the thoughts going through his head.

What the hell had he done?

In hindsight, it would have been a darn good idea to work out his feelings for Mia before he'd had sex with her.

Because of her past, she wasn't the strongest person and he had no right to play with her emotions. Heck, at a minimum he should have thought of their son. Mia was right. Sex did complicate things—and they didn't need that. They already had enough complications.

"I think you cured my claustrophobia," she whispered. "You did what a hoard of therapists hadn't been able to do. Thank you for that."

"You're welcome," he said because he didn't know what else to say.

She met his eyes again. "No matter what happens, this isn't going to cause me to have some mental setback. It's okay, Logan. It's *really* okay."

He frowned. "Are you reading my mind?"

The corner of her mouth lifted, but it wasn't exactly a smile of humor. "Mind-reading isn't necessary. You've got that trapped look in your eyes."

He immediately tried to change his expression. "Well, I don't feel trapped." But the problem was he didn't know how he felt. "Because of my line of work, I've spent most of my adult life avoiding serious relationships. I always wanted kids, but I didn't figure one would be in my future this soon."

She nodded. Because of her childhood trauma, she'd certainly done her share of avoiding relationships.

Tanner finished nursing and she put him on her shoulder to burp him. She leaned over and brushed a kiss on Logan's cheek. It wasn't a hot and lusty one, nor was it one of those mindless spousal pecks.

It had a goodbye feel to it.

And that bothered him.

"It's okay, Logan," Mia said, her voice light and feathery. "Having sex with me can mean as little as you want it to mean."

Hell, that bothered him, too. And then it riled him. "What—"

But that was as far as he got in what would no doubt be an argument because the phone rang. He'd brought his jeans into the bedroom, but since he'd discarded them on the floor, he had to get off the bed and fish through the pocket to retrieve his cell.

"McGrath," he snarled.

"It's Jason. There's a visitor for you here in the hotel lobby—Donnie Bishop."

Logan was certain that caused his scowl to deepen because Donnie Bishop should have been nowhere near the place. He pressed the speaker function so that Mia could hear the rest of the conversation.

"What does Bishop want?" Logan asked. He glanced at Mia. She was staring at the phone as if expecting to hear the worst.

"He has a package for you. I scanned it and it's not a bomb. He says it's a CD and that's what it appears to be."

Maybe it was the sample that Donnie had promised them. "Open it and verify that's what it is. And while you're doing that, let me talk to Donnie."

A moment later, the man came onto the line. "Logan, I have what you and I discussed at the prison and I'd like to give it to you in person."

"Well, we don't always get what we want, do we?" Because there was no way Logan was going to allow Donnie Bishop any-where near Mia and Tanner. "Now, tell me how the hell you found out where I was staying?"

But Logan immediately thought of the

meeting at the prison. The way Donnie had pulled Mia and him into a huddle so he could tell them to meet him in the parking lot. During that embrace, he could have put a transmitter on them.

"You planted another tracker somewhere on our clothes," Logan snarled.

"I wouldn't do that." There was a touch of sarcasm in his voice. Enough to confirm that Donnie had done just that. "Maybe I just have a nose for finding people."

"You're an SOB, you know that." But Logan silently added much harsher profanity. Not just for Donnie. But for himself. He should have checked their clothes; the shooting had distracted him.

He'd let himself get distracted too often lately.

"So?" Donnie asked. "Can I come up and have a beer and a man-to-man chat with you?"

"Not on your worthless life. Leave the disk with Cartwright and once I've listened to it, I'll be in touch with you."

Or better yet, he'd be in touch with the police.

"Oh, you'll want to hear more," Donnie insisted. "A lot more."

Logan hoped that was true. But while he was hoping that he also thought there might be evidence on that disk for the police to make an arrest. Of course, there was no way Donnie would incriminate himself. Still, there might be something to nail Genevieve or Royce and maybe one or both of them would incriminate Donnie. Logan wanted the man arrested for something.

"I sent your visitor on his way and I'm having hotel security monitor him to make sure he leaves the building." Jason said, coming back onto the line. "I'm on my way up to bring you the disk."

"Once you've dropped it off, make sure Donnie Bishop doesn't come back," Logan insisted.

Mia got up from the bed and placed Tanner in the bassinet. She also began to get dressed. What she didn't do was look at him.

Logan dressed, too, so he could go to the door and get the disk from Jason. He took his gun with him when he went to answer the knock.

Jason handed him the single silver CD that had "Careless Whispers" handwritten on it with a permanent marker. The plastic case covering the disk was wet.

"It's raining and sleeting," Jason let him know when Logan ran his index finger through the moisture. "There's a bad storm moving in tonight."

With the thick drapes closed, Logan hadn't been aware of the change of weather. But he had to wonder—why had Donnie braved the weather to get this recording to them? He could have had a courier bring it over.

Unless he had something more sinister in mind.

With Donnie, that wasn't too much of a stretch.

Logan thanked Jason for the CD, closed the door and locked it as quickly as he could. He only hoped that Donnie wasn't using the delivery of the recording as a ruse to try to get to them.

Mia came into the sitting room where he was putting the disk into the CD player in the entertainment unit. There was a hiss of static and then, as clear as a bell, he heard Genevieve's voice.

"I want this surrogate. She's the only one who's come in that looks like me. That's why I arranged to have her inseminated with that semen I got from Cryogen Labs."

Judging from her tone she was repeating the information or arguing with someone. Her voice was tight and adamant. And Genevieve was no doubt talking about Mia.

Mia walked closer, obviously disturbed with hearing the confirmation of Genevieve's plan.

A plan that had succeeded in creating a child.

"I can't go along with this," someone on the disk said. Logan easily recognized that voice, too. It was none other than Donnie Bishop.

"Oh, but you will go along with it," Genevieve demanded. "As a favor to my father. You know these people here at Brighton. You know how to make this work for me."

Here at Brighton. So, they were at the clinic for this little chat. And if Genevieve had already started the whole surrogacy process, then it was…approximately what date? Early April maybe, since that was the month of Mia's insemination. Or perhaps it was even May and Mia was already pregnant.

Maybe there'd be a surveillance video to confirm this meeting. Logan wouldn't mind seeing the pair's body language to try to determine if anything other than the obvious was going on. It was possible that Donnie was simply using this recording to make Genevieve look as guilty as possible. Of course, Genevieve *was* guilty, but Logan wasn't convinced she was in on this alone.

"Favors don't extend this far," Donnie informed her. "I won't help you kidnap a woman and steal her baby. My advice? If you want your boyfriend back, a baby's not the way to do it, anyway. Try liberal amounts of tequila and some scented massage oils. That works on me."

"Maybe you don't understand what I'm saying." Genevieve again. She was really riled now. "This isn't a request. One way or another, I *will* get a baby."

"Surrogacy is *sooo* messy," Donnie said.

Logan remembered the man saying that before in reference to George Devereux. "Especially when there are much easier ways to go about this. Let me give you someone to contact. She recently moved into the home for unwed mothers that's near here. Her name is Collena Drake and she's pregnant."

Logan hadn't expected to hear Collena's name pop up in this particular conversation. Of course, he knew Collena had worked undercover at Brighton, but he hadn't thought she'd used her real name.

"So?" Genevieve fired back.

"So, Collena Drake can assist you in finding a suitable child to adopt from the home, and then you can always fake the DNA results for your boyfriend. If you need any help with that, just let me know. I have friends who have friends who work in DNA labs."

Genevieve didn't answer right away. "I can trust this woman, Collena Drake?"

Donnie laughed. "As much as you can trust anyone around here. But I'm going to give you some leverage when it comes to her. Leverage that will force her to cooperate in case she gives you any resistance."

"What kind of leverage?"

"The best kind. Collena Drake is an undercover cop of sorts. Her assignment hasn't been sanctioned by SAPD. She's a renegade. Keep that hush-hush, just between us. If the clinic director finds out, she'll murder Sgt. Drake and I wouldn't want that to happen. I might need a cop if the Feds investigate this place. Go to Collena Drake. Put in your baby request. Pay her well. And she'll stay quiet because she won't have a choice."

That was it. The recording ended.

Logan and Mia stood there in silence. Letting it all sink in. Logan not believing what the heck he'd just heard.

"Was Collena working for Donnie?" Mia asked.

"No." But Logan didn't like the sliver of doubt that he felt creep into his mind. "Besides, Donnie could have doctored this recording. I won't know if it's authentic until I've sent it to the lab for testing."

Donnie Bishop is a slimy jerk, Logan reminded himself. *Collena Drake is a former cop.* If it came down to it, he'd trust Collena.

Still, it wouldn't hurt to verify a few things.

He took his cell phone and called Collena's room at the hospital. It was late, but hopefully she'd still be awake. It took four rings before anyone answered.

And the person on the other end of the line definitely wasn't Collena Drake.

It was Roger Dade, the team member he'd assigned to guard Collena at the hospital.

"This is Logan. Where is she?"

"I was just about to call you. Collena's gone."

Logan felt his stomach tighten. "Gone where?"

"I don't know. And I'm not sure how she got out of her room. I didn't see her leave."

His stomach tightened even more. "So someone could have kidnapped her?"

"Maybe. But it doesn't look that way, Logan."

"Then what the hell does it look like?" But Logan instinctively knew he wasn't going to like the answer.

Roger Dade cleared his throat. "It looks as if she sneaked out. As to why she'd do that—it's anyone's guess."

Oh, Logan had a guess, several of them, in fact.

And none of them were good.

Chapter Fourteen

"Collena left the hospital?" Mia repeated after hearing Logan's account of what'd happened. "Why would she do something like that?"

Logan stayed quiet a moment, the only sound was the partially frozen rain battering against the trio of windows in the sitting room. "I'm not sure."

He tried to call Collena's cell phone again, but through the tiny speaker, Mia heard the call go directly to voice mail, just as the other calls had done. The woman apparently wasn't answering tonight. Mia could tell from Logan's stiff posture and tight jaw that he was not happy about this latest development.

She wasn't exactly happy about it, either.

They already had enough unsolved riddles without adding this one.

"Something obviously went wrong at the hospital," Logan mumbled. "That's why Collena left. That's the only explanation for it."

"But is she even medically okay to be away from her doctors?"

He shook his head. "I doubt it, which tells us something. Whatever happened must have been serious enough for her to risk her health by leaving."

Mia didn't like the obvious conclusion of that. "She might have thought she was in imminent danger. But then, why wouldn't she have just gone to your team member since he was in the hall guarding her?"

His jaw tightened even more. "I have no idea. But I'll find out."

He tried Collena's number again and then cursed under his breath when she still didn't answer. Logan had his thumb poised over the button to redial her number again, but another call rang through.

"McGrath," he answered immediately, using the speaker function so Mia could hear.

"It's me."

Not Collena, but Donnie Bishop. Mia groaned. Now was not the time for another dose of Donnie.

"Tell me about Collena Drake."

"Tell me what you know about my frickin' house," Donnie countered. "Who the hell set fire to it?"

Surprised and concerned, Mia walked closer and sank down on the sofa next to Logan. She touched his arm and rubbed gently. It didn't seem to help. His muscles stayed tight and knotted.

"I don't know who set fire to your house," Logan answered, after taking a weary breath. "But please tell me you didn't have your recordings stashed there."

"Oh, they were there, all right, in a hidden floor vault in the basement. I'm still on my way there, but according to the police, it looks as if everything down in that basement was destroyed. I'm guessing that the intense heat would have melted the disks. A coincidence? I don't think so, and that's why I want some answers from you."

Mia squeezed her eyes shut and tried not

to curse. Those recordings were their best chance at an arrest and now they were gone.

And no, it wasn't a coincidence.

"Now, here's the question, Logan," Donnie continued. "Did you tell Genevieve that I'd given you the sample of our conversation?"

"No. I haven't had time. In fact, I just finished listening to it about a half hour ago. Do the police suspect arson in your house fire?"

"You bet your butt they do. According to their preliminary search, someone doused the basement with accelerant. A lot of it. And since I was at your hotel dropping off the recording, I obviously wasn't home to stop this idiotic firebug or to call 911."

"But you suspect Genevieve?" Logan clarified.

"Of course. Who else?"

Genevieve was a solid suspect, but Mia had to wonder—could Collena Drake have done this? After all, that recording insinuated that she was a dirty cop. Of course, in that recording Donnie was the one who'd accused Collena of being dirty and Donnie wasn't exactly a trustworthy guy. He could have made those accusations or even doctored the recording to make himself sound more innocent than he really was.

Donnie was droning on about Logan having to do something to stop all of this nonsense when Mia heard the slight click.

"Sorry," Logan said immediately to Donnie. "I have to go. I have another call coming in. But good luck looking for that arsonist." The sarcasm drowned his voice. "When or if you find the person responsible, let me know."

Mia stood, went to the bar to pour herself a glass of mineral water. However, she stopped when she heard the caller's voice on Logan's speakerphone.

Logan caught Mia's gaze before he answered the call. The frustration was still there in his eyes, but there was a small amount of relief. Mia felt it, too. Because until she'd heard Collena's voice, she'd had a niggling fear in the back of her mind that the woman might be dead.

"Collena," Logan greeted her. "I've been trying to reach you."

"Yes, I saw your name on my caller ID, but I couldn't answer the phone right then. I couldn't be sure that no one was following me."

Well, that sounded ominous, but then Mia hadn't expected Collena to deliver good news.

"Where are you?" Logan asked.

"I'd rather not say, just in case the line isn't secure." Her voice was shaky. "I found a tiny transmitter on my dinner tray, right there next to a carton of milk."

"Donnie," Logan mouthed.

Mia had to agree. Donnie had certainly been active in planting bugs and it wouldn't have been difficult to put one on a hospital tray.

"And then when the nurse opened the door to my room," Collena continued, "I thought I saw Royce Foreman lurking around in the hall. Since I knew I couldn't defend myself, I couldn't hang around and wait to see what he was going to do."

Logan groaned. "And that's why you left?"

"I got a really bad feeling, Logan. Like something horrible was about to happen.

The last time I ignored a feeling like that, someone tried to kill me at Brighton."

"My guard would have protected you," Logan reminded her.

"Maybe, but I couldn't stay in that room. And I knew I'd made the right decision about leaving when I heard about the fire."

That obviously grabbed his attention. "How did you hear about the fire?"

"I called my office. When no one answered, I phoned a colleague. He said that someone had set fire to the office and that everything inside was probably destroyed. That includes the hard copy files and some of the other evidence that the police had confiscated from Brighton."

Mia nearly laughed, not from humor, but from the insanity of it all.

Two fires in the same night.

And both had destroyed what could have been the evidence they needed to solve this case. It wasn't a coincidence. The person responsible was trying to cover their tracks.

"I have to go," Collena said. Her voice wasn't just shaky, it was weak. Mia was feeling so skeptical, however, that she had to wonder if it was all an act. Maybe Collena wasn't as weak from her injury as everyone thought. "I'll call you when I get a chance."

With that, Collena hung up, leaving Logan and Mia with more questions than ever.

Logan sat there quietly for several moments before he picked up the baby monitor that was positioned so he could see Tanner sleeping in his bassinet. Mia knew what he was thinking. The stakes were so high, and the person responsible for the danger just kept eluding them.

"Is Genevieve capable of setting two fires?" Mia asked.

Logan nodded. "But she also could have hired someone to do it so she wouldn't get her hands dirty."

"Or it could have been Royce who's responsible. After all, Collena said she thought she saw him in the hall at the hospital."

Neither of them stated the obvious: that Collena could have been mistaken.

Or lying.

She could have left the hospital to set fire to Donnie's house. But there was no motive for burning her own office. Just the opposite.

From what Mia had learned about her, Collena was obsessed with finding out the truth of what'd happened to her own baby. Even if she was dirty, she wouldn't have destroyed the very evidence that would help her with that search.

And that led them right back to Genevieve and Royce.

"We have the recording," Mia reminded him. "Do you think the police can do anything with it?"

"Man, I hope so." He put the baby monitor aside and went to the CD player to retrieve it. "I'll have one of my men drive it to the Ranger crime lab in Austin. There might be something we can use." Logan stood there staring at her. "You're exhausted. Why don't you go ahead to bed and get some rest while Tanner's sleeping? I'll wake you as soon as Jason's made the arrangements for us to leave."

She was beyond exhausted, but she was more interested in getting some things straight with Logan. Since they'd had sex, there seemed to be a distance between them. The problem was Mia didn't know if or how she should address it. Maybe this was

Logan's way of backing off, to give himself some time to think.

She certainly needed time.

Things had moved so fast between them and there were times, like now, when she felt as though they were on a speeding train that was about to jump the tracks.

She'd been the one to initiate sex and she didn't regret it. No, she could never regret it because it'd been one of the most memorable experiences of her life. But logically, she had to look at what this was going to do to them. And that's why she, too, needed to back off, to give them both some breathing room.

"Go ahead to bed," Logan insisted. He walked to her and slid his arm around her waist. He brushed a kiss on her temple. "I'll join you after I give this recording to Jason."

Just like that, her worries about derailing trains and breathing room vanished. The simple kiss, embrace and soft reassurance were stark reminders that she wasn't in control here.

Her heart was.

That should have scared her to death. But it didn't. This felt right.

And that's what scared her, because there was nothing she could do to change the course her heart was taking.

She was falling in love with Logan.

He kissed her again, easing her closer to him. And the closeness and the kiss stirred her need for him all over again.

Mia pulled back to meet his gaze and was on the verge of insisting he go ahead and give Jason the disk so he, too, could come back to bed.

But then, without warning, the lights went out. The room was suddenly pitch black.

"The storm," she whispered. "It must have knocked out the electricity."

Logan pulled away from her and she felt him fumble around for something. When her eyes adjusted to the darkness, she saw what he had picked up from the coffee table.

His gun.

Her breath stalled in her lungs.

Because she knew this might not be a power outage after all. The person who wanted them dead might be responsible.

"Go to Tanner," Logan ordered. "Stay there until you hear from me."

He didn't wait for her to respond. With his gun gripped in his hands, he hurried toward the suite door.

LOGAN BRACED HIMSELF for anything that might happen when he stepped from the suite and into the hall.

There was no chance he believed bad weather had knocked out the electricity. Not with their luck. Besides, the hotel would almost certainly have a backup generator, and since it hadn't kicked in Logan had to assume the worst.

The gunman had returned to finish what he'd started.

With his gun ready, Logan opened the suite door and checked the hall. Dorien was there, obviously alarmed. She too was armed and looked ready to do battle. Good. He needed all the help he could get.

"Go in the bedroom and wait with Mia and the baby," Logan instructed.

He waited until Dorien had done that before he ventured a few steps down the hall and away from the door.

"Jason?" Logan called out in the darkness.

"I'm here by the stairs. I want to make sure no one gets up here."

That was a start. "What happened? Why did the electricity go out?"

"The manager doesn't know yet. I just got off the phone with him and he's checking it out. I warned him that someone might have tampered with the main circuits."

Again, that was a good start, but it wasn't enough. Of course, nothing might be enough with Tanner and Mia in danger. "What about any other points of entry? I don't want anyone getting up here."

"The elevators aren't working. There's a service entrance at the end of this corridor, but even if anyone comes up through those stairs, they'd still have to get past me to get to you."

"No one gets past you," Logan let him know. It wasn't a suggestion. Jason was well trained and would have to use that training to stop the threat. "How many men do we have in the hotel?"

"Five. Me, you, Dorien and two more downstairs. Those two are posted by the service entrance and the stairs."

So all points of entry were covered.

In theory.

But Logan had to be ready just in case someone had found another way to gain access.

There was only one window, located at the end of the hall. Logan went to it and checked outside. It confirmed what he already suspected. The River Walk was all lit up. No power outages there, which meant whoever cut the power was already in the building and had disconnected the backup generator.

Hell.

He did not want to put Mia and Tanner through this again.

There was another problem with the window, too. Not just this particular one either, but *all* the windows. With the power out, Logan automatically assumed that their shooter might make a direct attack to the room, but cutting the lights could be a ploy; the attack could come from a sniper positioned in the hotel on the other side of the River Walk.

That's why he needed to remind Mia to stay away from the windows.

However, before he could do that, there was a slight sound, and Logan whirled around. Ready to fire.

"It's me," he heard Mia say as she opened the suite door. "Your cell phone rang and I answered it. It's Royce Foreman, and he says it's important."

Logan cursed again, automatically suspicious. Was this call some kind of ploy? Or maybe Royce knew what was going on.

So that she wouldn't have to come out into the hall and potentially be in the line of fire from that window, Logan went to her.

"Make sure you stay away from the windows," Logan whispered.

She nodded and handed him the phone. "Dorien and I moved Tanner and his bassinet into the bathroom. There aren't any windows there."

And that meant he was as safe as Logan could manage.

He hated that it didn't seem nearly enough.

"McGrath," Logan answered. He didn't launch into accusations or a verbal attack, though he wanted to do just that. He waited to see what Royce considered "important" enough to call him about.

"The police questioned me again," Royce started. "About the shooting at the prison. I was in that dingy little interrogation room for more than two hours. They did that because you told them that I might have been the one who did it."

"Were you?" Logan didn't take his attention off the corridor. He wanted to make sure that no one came up either set of stairs and got past Jason. He also eased Mia several inches back into the suite.

"No. And don't bring up that lunacy about me wanting revenge for you rescuing that woman in South America. Killing you wouldn't get me those shares and I prefer to concentrate my energies on my business."

"I wish I could believe that," Logan said, certain that he sounded disinterested. "But I don't. And I don't have time to rehash this now."

"You're focusing on the wrong person, Logan, and that's a deadly mistake."

That caused Logan to pause a moment. "You mean Donnie or Genevieve? Oh, I suspect them, too. But that doesn't let you off the hook. For starters, why were you at the hospital earlier and why were you skulking around outside Collena Drake's room?"

Logan figured that Royce would launch into another adamant denial.

He didn't.

"I wanted to see Collena. Because I think she's linked to all of these attempts to kill you."

Logan groaned. "Have you been talking to Donnie Bishop?"

"No." Royce's answer was quick, but maybe that was because he'd anticipated the question and was ready.

"Then why would you think Collena is connected with the attempts to kill me?" And why were both Donnie and Royce so eager to accuse a former cop of wrongdoing?

Probably to cover their own guilt.

At least, Logan hoped that's what it was. He hated the doubts that kept creeping into his mind, but he was a man alive because of doubts. Because he questioned things that most people would have considered safe.

Was that what he was doing now?

"After you wrongfully accused me of the shooting and the car explosion," Royce continued, "I did some checking. Over the past five months, someone has attempted to kill several of the people associated with the Brighton Birthing Center."

"I know about that." Logan, too, had researched them. In all four cases, the culprits had been caught. "That doesn't mean Collena had anything to do with those attempts."

"Well, someone did and it's not me. I want my name cleared."

"You should talk to Genevieve about that," Logan let him know. "If you want to do some finger pointing, her direction is always the best place to start."

"Genevieve and I aren't on speaking terms anymore. I saw how she looked at you at the prison and I confronted her about it. It's over between us. She lied to me—she's still in love with you, Logan."

"Hardly. She's obsessed with the fact that she can't have me. That's not love."

And this conversation was going nowhere.

He was also starting to get the feeling that Royce might have ulterior motives for this call.

Was Royce using some kind of signal from Logan's phone to pinpoint their location inside the hotel?

Equipment like that wasn't easy to come by, but it was too big of a risk to take.

He didn't say goodbye to Royce and didn't give him any indication that he was hanging up. Logan merely punched the end call button and turned to tell Mia that he wanted her inside the bathroom. For an extra measure of security, he tossed his phone on the floor so he'd put some distance between it and them. Once he had her safely tucked away, he wanted to give his phone a more thorough examination.

He gently took her arm and in the darkness caught her gaze. "I just need to make sure you're safe," he whispered.

She nodded. Stepped back.

Just as an explosion tore through the corridor.

Chapter Fifteen

One second Mia was standing and the next second Logan had shoved her back onto the floor of the suite. It wasn't a moment too soon because along with that deafening blast came a cloud of dust and debris.

It took a moment to regain her breath and for her brain to register what was happening. Someone had set off an explosive.

With her heart ramming against her chest, Mia looked at Logan to make sure he hadn't been hurt. It was difficult to see him in the murky, dark room, but his catlike movement to get back to the door told her that he was probably okay. And he was ready to strike back at whoever was responsible for this. Which made her think—just how much damage had been done to the hotel?

And to whom?

"Tanner," she managed to say.

"Check on him," Logan insisted. But he wouldn't go. *Couldn't* go. Because she knew he had to stand guard to make sure the bomber didn't get into the room with them.

Mia raced through the sitting room and into the bedroom. Their son had to be okay. He just had to be.

Thankfully, the bathroom was at the end of the suite away from the explosion, and there were no signs of dust and debris in here.

"Is Tanner okay?" Mia called out. She listened for any sounds and couldn't hear anything. No crying. No sound of any movement.

That didn't make Mia feel better.

"He's fine," Dorien assured her.

Mia was so overwhelmed with relief that tears sprang to her eyes.

Dorien opened the bathroom door just a fraction. She had her gun drawn and was obviously ready to defend Tanner. "What's going on?"

Mia peeked in to make sure Tanner was

okay. He was. "Someone set off a bomb. Stay put until we can sort things out."

"Do you need my help?" Dorien asked.

"No." Mia motioned toward the sitting room. "But I need to check on Logan. I won't be long. And I'll keep the hotel-room door in my line of sight to make sure that no one gets inside here."

Mia rushed back into the sitting area. She pulled in her breath and smelled the smoke. "Is there a fire?" she called out to Logan. The possibility of it made her heart beat even faster.

"I don't think so. I think it might just be sparks from the explosion." Logan made his way just outside the corridor. "How's Tanner?"

"He's okay. I don't think the explosive even woke him up." She hoped it stayed that way for a while.

And then Mia heard a sound she didn't want to hear.

Someone was moaning in pain. It wasn't loud. But she could clearly hear it. For one terrifying moment, she thought it might be Tanner or Dorien. But this sound wasn't coming from the suite.

It was coming from the corridor.

"Jason?" Logan shouted.

Oh, God. With everything going on, she'd forgotten about Jason Cartwright. The man had been at the end of the hall near the elevators and even though she didn't know exactly where the explosion had originated, Jason had likely been right in the path.

"Stay here," Logan warned her. "And just in case someone hasn't already done it, try to use the hotel phone to call 911 and request an ambulance."

Mia hadn't thought her fears and concerns could get any worse, but they did when she saw Logan move in the direction of the explosion. He was obviously going to check on Jason. She knew it had to be done, but she hated that Logan had to risk his life for it to happen.

She covered her mouth and nose with her hand to keep from breathing in the smoke and dust and went to the phone on the table near the sofa.

There was no dial tone.

Mia didn't give up. She remembered Logan tossing his cell phone on the floor in the corridor. She didn't know why he'd done that, but maybe if the debris hadn't covered it, she'd still be able to find it.

Moving cautiously, she peeked around the doorframe to make sure it was safe to go out there, but all she could see was the darkness. At the other end of the hall, there were sounds of Logan moving around, and she could even hear voices. Hopefully, that meant that Jason was all right.

Stooping, she ran her hands over the floor to search for the phone. Her fingers encountered something. A chunk of plaster, she realized, and it was a stark reminder of just how close they'd come to being in the path of that blast. After all, only seconds earlier, they'd been in that very corridor.

"How's Jason?" she called out to Logan while she still searched for the phone.

"Alive," was all Logan said. "But he needs a doctor—fast. He's hurt bad."

Mia was afraid he was going to say that. She coughed and swished her hand in front of her face, hoping to clear the smoke and dust so she could breathe. "The hotel phone isn't working. I'm trying to find your cell phone now."

Frantically, she tossed aside more chunks of plaster and wood and wished she had her own cell phone. Unfortunately, she'd had to leave it at her house in the aftermath of the other explosion—the one that'd destroyed Logan's car.

This explosion had already done far more damage than the first one and if she didn't find that phone to call for an ambulance, Jason might die.

But Mia froze.

She detected some movement at the end of the corridor where Logan and Jason were.

She had a sickening feeling in the pit of her stomach that it was neither Jason nor Logan.

There was a thump, but she couldn't distinguish what had happened. Maybe, just maybe, it was Logan repositioning Jason so he could tend to his injuries.

"Logan?" Mia asked, terrified of what she would or wouldn't hear. "Are you okay?"

He didn't answer. Not right away.

"Genevieve," he said.

Slowly, Mia stood and tried to pick through the dark corridor to see why Logan had said the woman's name. But Mia was afraid she knew why.

Mercy, was Genevieve at the end of that corridor? And was she holding a gun on Logan? Mia refused to think beyond that. Genevieve hadn't hurt Logan. Or worse.

And she'd better not try.

Anger surged through her and Mia wrapped her hand around a thick strip of wood that the explosion had displaced. It was part of a door frame and, if necessary, Mia was going to use it to stop Genevieve from doing anything to Logan or the rest of them.

There was more movement, more voices that she couldn't understand. A woman's voice. And that was Mia's cue to get moving, as well. Because of the debris and a partially collapsed wall, she couldn't exactly run through the corridor, but she hurried.

She had to get to Logan in time.

The old nightmares returned. Of the night she'd raced through the house to try to save her parents. Only to find them dead. Only to find herself under attack from their killers. As always, the images were brutal. She could taste the fear in her mouth.

But that fear didn't stop her.

Nor did the threat of a panic attack.

She had only one goal. To get to Logan. And nothing was going to stop her.

Mia maneuvered around the collapsed wall and finally saw the two shadowy figures. There was another person or something shaped like a person lying on the floor. Jason, probably. And that meant Logan and Genevieve were standing.

Did the woman have a gun, and was she holding it on Logan? Maybe Genevieve had managed to sneak up on him while he was trying to take care of Jason. Unfortunately, that was a good theory because neither of them was moving. Maybe that meant Genevieve had a gun pointed to Logan's head.

Mia didn't call out Logan's name. She tried not to make a sound, just in case it wasn't too late to have the element of surprise on her side.

With the wood strip gripped in her hand, Mia charged forward.

Only to come to a complete stop.

When one of the shadowy figures dropped to the floor.

Her heart dropped, too, and she heard herself cry out Logan's name.

"I'm okay," Logan told her.

She didn't believe him because her mind was still racing with so many thoughts of what Genevieve might have done to him.

Mia stopped and forced her eyes to focus in the darkness. She finally saw Logan. He was standing. But he was the only one of the three who was. Jason was on the floor to his left. He was moving, his chest pumping as if he were fighting for every breath.

And directly in front of Logan was Genevieve.

Not moving. Not breathing.

Judging from her limp body, the woman was dead.

LOGAN HEARD MIA yell for him, but before he could answer, Genevieve staggered forward and collapsed against him. She was shivering and clutching her chest. He saw the blood spatters on her clothes and face.

God, what had happened to her?

"What were you doing in what's left of that stairwell?" he asked. "You set the bomb, didn't you?"

She moved her mouth, trying to speak. But it sounded as if she were drowning in gravel.

Mia raced toward them, and he looked up to catch her gaze so she could see he was all right. The eye contact was brief because both of them turned their attention back to Genevieve.

"Lo-gan," Genevieve mumbled. "I'm sorry."

The last syllable had hardly left her mouth when she went limp. There was no final breath. No other sounds. He saw the life drain from her body.

Logan stood there, trying to absorb what's just happened, and even after several long moments, he still didn't know what was going on.

How had Genevieve gotten onto the stairs of the service entrance? He'd had a man guarding them from the lobby since long before the explosion.

Unless she'd slipped past earlier, and then…what? Set the explosion? That made sense. Well, it made sense as much as it could with Genevieve involved.

Mia stooped and put her fingers to Genevieve's neck, checking for a pulse.

She wouldn't find one.

Genevieve had literally staggered out of what was left of the service stairwell and collapsed against Logan. She'd tried to speak. But Logan hadn't understood what she'd tried to tell him. That's because within moments after coming from that stairwell, she'd dropped dead.

"She's not breathing," Mia whispered.

Her voice was shaky, and that gave Logan something else to be concerned with. All of this might launch Mia into a panic attack.

"I thought she was going to try to kill you," Mia said, standing.

"I thought the same thing." He touched her arm, just to let her know that he was there in case she needed him. "Genevieve must have been injured in the explosion."

She lifted her eyes to meet his. "So, you didn't do this to her?"

He shook his head. "I think she might have set the explosion. Maybe it went off before she could get out of here."

Mia's breath shuttered. "And if so, that means she was trying to kill us."

"Yeah."

Logan left it at that, because they both already knew she had motive. Though he'd never, never understand the obsession Genevieve had had with him. She'd endangered a child that she was partly responsible for creating simply so she could get back at him. Later, he'd try to come to terms with that, but right now, he had a more pressing matter.

Jason needed an ambulance.

"Did you find the cell phone?" Logan asked Mia.

"No. It's still back there by the suite door, somewhere on the floor."

He leaned down and checked Jason. Unlike Genevieve, his pulse was steady and strong. He was also unconscious. But judging from what Jason had told him right after Logan got to him, the man had some broken ribs. Maybe even a collapsed lung. If all that weren't bad enough, he was bleeding from a deep gash on his arm. He was losing way too much blood.

"You think you can put a tourniquet or something on Jason's arm?" Logan asked Mia.

She nodded, though she didn't look certain. He could understand why. A dead woman. An injured man. This had to be giving her some serious flashbacks of the death of her parents. That's why he had to hurry. He didn't want her alone any longer than absolutely necessary.

Logan started to make his way in that direction when the lights came on. Not the overheads, but the smaller light sconces on the walls. Someone had obviously turned on the backup generator.

And that gave Logan his first real look at what had happened.

It looked like chaos. There was debris everywhere, scattered along the entire length of the corridor. But only one guest room had been damaged. The one closest to the explosion. Thankfully, the impact hadn't gotten anywhere near the suite where Tanner was.

He needed to get all of them out of the

hotel. Even though the threat from Genevieve was over—permanently—he didn't know if the hotel structure had been compromised by the explosion. Plus, he didn't want Mia and Tanner to have to be in this mess any longer than necessary.

Logan hurried past the debris. He needed that phone, though he was almost certain that by now someone in his crew or the hotel staff had called the police. Still, he could speed things up by requesting an ambulance.

He dug through the chunks of drywall and finally located the cell phone. He turned it on, staring at the screen, waiting until he could press in 911.

"Logan," he heard Mia say.

He immediately heard the panic in her voice and wondered if this was all too much for her. He shouldn't have left her with Genevieve's body.

"I'm here," he said, standing so he could go to her.

But Logan only managed a step before he stopped in his tracks.

Mia was there, at the end of the corridor. Genevieve and Jason were still on the floor. But there was someone standing behind Mia.

And that someone had a gun pressed to her head.

Chapter Sixteen

Mia hadn't heard the footsteps until it was too late.

The arm snapped around her neck. Too fast for her to do anything to stop it.

Just as fast, someone dragged her to her feet. Before she could even make a sound, she felt the cold hard barrel of a handgun jam against her right temple.

And the fear and the adrenaline sliced through her.

She struggled, shoving her weight about the person, but the chokehold only tightened until she couldn't breathe.

Mia had no idea who her attacker was, and she couldn't look back because the person was literally holding her in place with a choke hold and that gun. She managed to say Logan's name, though she didn't know how. There wasn't much air getting through her windpipe and she thought this person might kill her where she stood.

She saw Logan then. She watched his face as he registered what was happening to her. And she hated that she'd said his name. Mia had meant it as a warning. So that he could try to get away, but in hindsight, that was a stupid and possibly fatal mistake.

Because Logan would never leave her with a killer.

She braced herself for the flashbacks. For a full-blown panic attack.

But it didn't come.

Instead, there was a greater fear, far worse than anything that had happened in her past. Because if this killer took out both Logan and her, then he or she might go after Tanner. Their son might be hurt.

Logan walked toward her. Or rather, he stormed toward her. But her attacker merely rammed the gun harder against her temple and the chokehold tightened until Mia started gasping for air.

That stopped Logan, and he lowered his

gun to his side when the attacker motioned for him to do so.

"You should have both died in the explosion," her attacker said. "I miscalculated which room you were in. I guess the maid I bribed was misinformed."

The moment she heard his words, she had no trouble recognizing the voice.

Donnie Bishop.

"The police will be here soon," Donnie added.

"Too soon for you to escape," Logan insisted. He inched toward them.

Donnie made a sound of disagreement. "The elevators are blocked. Stairwells, too, because I fixed each door so that they won't open. It'll take them a while to get up here. By then, I'll be gone. And so will you, *literally.* Say goodbye to him, Mia."

Mia frantically shook her head and considered begging Donnie to rethink this, but it wouldn't do any good. He'd obviously come to kill them.

But why?

She'd understood Genevieve's motive, perhaps even Royce's if he truly had wanted revenge against Logan. But Donnie had been the last on her list of suspects.

"Was Genevieve your partner?" Logan asked, probably to stall Donnie's attempt to execute them.

She felt Donnie move slightly, and she thought he might have looked down at the lifeless woman.

"What a bimbo," he grumbled. "I helped her with the surrogacy because she paid me an obscene amount of money and because she wasn't supposed to tell a soul. You see how well she kept that promise. But she works out very well to be scapegoat, don't you think? She'll get the blame for your deaths. And speaking of which, it's time to die. I bet the police are already in the building and are trying to figure out how to get up here."

Donnie was saying all the right things to make him sound like a cold-blooded killer, but because he was practically wrapped around her, Mia could feel him trembling. He was scared, too, and killing someone face-to-face wasn't nearly as easy as he'd probably thought it would be.

"Let Mia go," Logan said, taking another step forward. Mia could see his hand tense on his gun. His finger was still on the trigger. "You have no reason to kill her."

"I beg to differ. Between the two of you, you can put me in jail with your testimony. That's why I've been after you two."

Logan huffed. "You're actually going to kill us to avoid jail time?"

"A *long* jail time. Women were murdered at Brighton, and I knew about it. I even covered up evidence. Eventually Collena Drake would have discovered that and she would have had you two to fill in the rest so you could all testify against me."

"So you plan to kill Collena, too?"

"Once I'm done here. She shouldn't be hard to find. A wounded ex-cop without a lot of friends won't have a lot of places she can go. Don't," Donnie warned when Logan came even closer.

"I can't just let you kill her," Logan said.

"There's nothing you or I can do about it."

Oh yes, there was. Mia didn't know what exactly, but she wasn't just going to stand there and let him kill both Logan and her.

She thought of her son again and fixed the image of him in her head. Tanner couldn't lose both of his parents. She wouldn't let him go through what had happened to her. Not when she could do something to stop it.

Logan's index finger tensed on the trigger. Donnie tensed, too. She felt his stance change slightly. There was no more trembling.

He was within seconds of pulling that trigger.

Mia didn't think beyond doing something, though she really didn't have a plan. Moving as fast as she could, she ducked down her head and in the same motion, she rammed her elbow into Donnie's stomach.

It worked. Sort of.

He still fired the shot, but because she'd moved, it didn't hit her. However, her heart nearly stopped when she considered where the bullet could have gone.

"Logan!" she called out.

She dropped to the ground and tried to catch a glimpse of him, to make sure he was all right. But she wasn't able to do that because Donnie latched on to her hair and tried to drag her back in front of him.

He was strong, much stronger than she was, and she couldn't catch her breath. She was losing the battle until Donnie shoved the gun against her neck.

Right on the scars.

That was a huge mistake for him to make.

Because it didn't make her weak. She didn't want to surrender. She wanted to fight back. It wasn't just raw adrenaline that slammed through her. There was fury and rage. She was not going to go through this again.

Mia used the force from her forearm to knock the gun away from her throat.

Donnie fired again. But she didn't try to maneuver herself away from him. Instead, she launched herself at him. Mia scratched at his face, hitting him and latching on to any part of him that she could claw or grab.

Donnie still managed to fire again.

She braced herself for the sensation of being shot, or worse, but the only thing she felt was someone pulling her from behind.

Logan.

He tore her away from Donnie, pushing her to the side. She fell against Jason.

And since she was no longer standing, that cleared the path for Logan to go after Donnie.

If Logan was hurt, she certainly couldn't see any sign of it. And like her, he'd worked himself into a rage. But unlike her, he had the size and the strength to do something. He slammed his fist into Donnie's face.

Donnie staggered back. Landing hard against what was left of the service exit door. He nearly fell back into the gaping hole.

Then Donnie lifted his gun and aimed it at Logan.

Logan did the same.

Mia didn't have time to shout for Logan to get down. She didn't have time to do anything.

Donnie dived back into the open space behind him.

The relief was instant. Donnie hadn't shot Logan. But that relief was short-lived. Because she didn't hear Donnie crash into anything. Nor was there the sound of him falling down the steps.

Just the opposite.

She could hear him running away.

Escaping.

And if that happened, this nightmare would start all over again. Logan, Tanner and she would never be safe.

Logan obviously knew that, as well, because much to Mia's horror, he raced into the stairwell after the man.

LOGAN DIDN'T STOP and think.

He did what he knew he had to do, and what he had to do was go after Donnie.

If Donnie had told the truth about the blocked stairwells and elevator, Logan couldn't count on help from the police or his own crew. They might not be able to get through whatever obstacles Donnie had set in time to stop him from escaping.

Logan raced into the service stairwell and stomped through the debris left from the explosion. He heard Donnie. Not in the stairwell below, but above.

The man was headed to the roof where he probably had an escape route all planned out. Well, Logan couldn't let him go through with that plan. Donnie had to be stopped.

Logan barreled up the steps, taking them

two at a time. Or rather trying to. The pain was instant and it rifled through him until the muscles in his leg knotted. If he'd been a hundred percent, this wouldn't have been much of a match. But as it was, he was going to have to muster every bit of determination he could to put an end to this.

And then he heard something he didn't want to hear.

Footsteps coming from below him.

Cursing and praying he was wrong about what he would see, he glanced down.

He spotted Mia one flight of stairs away.

She wasn't looking at the weapon, but she had Jason's gun gripped in her hand. And that wasn't all. She didn't seem panicked. Or afraid. She looked determined.

Logan wanted no part of that.

Because her determination could get her killed.

"Go back," he warned her.

She frantically shook her head. "No, I won't. You need help."

That was true, but he didn't want help from her. He wanted her safe, and that wouldn't happen if she was anywhere near Donnie.

"Go to the suite," he ordered. And then he played dirty pool. "Think of Tanner. He needs you."

"I am thinking of him," she insisted. "I'm thinking of you, too. I'm thinking of all of us."

Logan cursed, but he couldn't take the time to argue with her. Judging from the sound of Donnie's steps, the man was almost to the top. Logan's best chance was to outrun Mia and hope to have everything resolved by the time she caught up with him.

It was a lofty goal.

Especially since each step was agony.

Still, he forced his body to do what it didn't want to do. He kept running. He kept forcing himself to move up those stairs.

Then, Logan heard the door slam at the top of the stairs.

Hell. That wasn't a good sound. Because it meant Donnie had made it to the roof and was likely on the last leg of his escape route.

Logan kicked things up a notch and turned the corner of the last stairwell. He spotted the door that would no doubt lead to the roof.

He also spotted the shadow.

A man's shadow.

Logan's mind had just enough time to register that this was a trick, that Donnie hadn't indeed gone out that door but was waiting to ambush him. Logan dived to the floor just in the nick of time.

The bullet that Donnie fired slammed into the concrete-block wall just above Logan's head.

Before Logan could fully regain his position and re-aim his gun, Donnie launched himself at him. He came down those steps, tackling Logan, and the impact sent him hard into that same concrete that the bullet had struck. Donnie didn't stop there. He rammed his knee into Logan's injured leg.

The pain was instant.

It knifed through Logan, knocking the breath out of him. And in the back of his mind, he knew that his injury had been his fatal flaw. It'd weakened him and given his opponent an advantage that he shouldn't have.

Logan expected Donnie to finish the attack. He expected Donnie to shoot him.

And there was a shot.

It blasted through the stairwell, echoing through the hollow space.

But the shot Logan heard didn't come from Donnie.

It came from below them in the stairwell.

Logan glanced down and saw Mia. She had Jason's gun raised in the air, and the bullet she'd fired had gone into the ceiling. She had her eyes closed, terrified of the gun she'd just fired.

Donnie immediately honed in Mia and Logan could tell the moment the man spotted her. He could also tell that Donnie was about to make Mia his main target.

The brief distraction that Mia had created was all that Logan needed.

When Donnie shifted to re-aim his gun at Mia, Logan drew back his fist. He put everything he had into it and his punch landed hard against Donnie's face. So hard that Logan heard a bone snap in the man's jaw.

Donnie staggered back.

Logan didn't give him any chance to use his gun. He tried to knock it from his hand and shoved him against the wall. Then he did it again. The second time did the trick. Donnie's eyes rolled back in his head and his gun dropped to the floor.

And so did Donnie.

Chapter Seventeen

It was chaos again.

Mia could hear the frantic movement and voices in the hotel corridor. The police had finally broken through the magnetized locking mechanisms that Donnie had attached to all the doors and the elevator.

Along with an ambulance, the police and some members of Logan's team had arrived, all of them rushing into the building and onto the damaged second floor. Everyone was scrambling to make sure there were no other injuries and no other explosives.

Once they were certain of that, they would be evacuated. Probably not Logan, though. Since he'd knocked Donnie unconscious, he'd stayed in intense combat mode and had ordered her back to the suite. She'd complied, mainly because she wanted to check on Tanner and because she wanted to get away from Donnie, the man who'd created the horrible chaos that'd nearly gotten them killed.

Mia sank down onto the suite floor just outside the bathroom where Dorien and Tanner were still tucked away. Tanner was asleep. How, Mia didn't know. But her son hadn't even stirred amid the explosion and the ensuing fight.

A fight they'd won.

She was too worried about Logan to appreciate that now, but she would later.

It was over. Donnie had been arrested and the threat was gone. Of course, that led her to another question—where would she go?

Mia was still asking herself that when she heard footsteps. Her heartbeat spiked. Her body went on alert. But she soon saw that it wasn't a threat.

Logan walked into the suite. Correction—he limped, just as he'd done on the stairwell. Mia got up and hurried to him. He didn't resist when she slipped her arm around his waist and helped him to the bed. She didn't miss his grimace of pain.

"You need a doctor," she insisted.

He caught her when she tried to pull back and face him. Instead, he pulled her closer. "No. Right now, you're what I need."

That took some of the fight out of her. Mia melted against him.

"How's Tanner?" he asked.

"Sleeping."

Logan reached over and for a moment she thought he was going to hold her hand, but he didn't. He took the gun away from her.

A gun she hadn't even remembered she was holding.

A sound of amusement jumped in her throat. Here she was, a person with a diagnosed phobia of guns who hadn't even been aware she was holding one.

He placed the weapon on the night table next to the bed. "The police will need to take it since you fired a shot."

Of course, they would. Mia stared at the gun and wondered why she'd let something like that have so much control over her. But that was the past. It wouldn't control her any longer.

Just minutes earlier she'd come face-to-face with a horrible fear—losing Logan. Everything else in her life suddenly seemed very manageable.

"How's Jason?" she asked.

"He'll be fine. The medics think he has a concussion, probably some cracked ribs, but they don't think it's anything too serious." He turned toward her. "You saved my life."

"You've saved mine too many times to count." She kissed his cheek. "Why did Donnie do this? Was it really only because he didn't want us to be able to testify against him?"

Logan nodded. "And apparently he was working alone when he came after Collena, you and me. I heard him tell the police that he'd lured Genevieve here with the promise that he'd help her get revenge, but that he planned to set her up to take the blame. He insists that her death was an accident."

"Well, that bomb wasn't an accident so he can be arrested for attempted murder."

"That and a whole lot more, including the

crimes he committed at Brighton. And I believe he set the fires at both his house and Collena's office, figuring that would take care of any witnesses or evidence against him."

"So he did all of this so he wouldn't have to go to jail." Mia shook her head. "He risked our lives for that."

"But he didn't win," Logan reminded her. "I think I also figured out how Genevieve found us at my house. Donnie had already planted the bug in the diaper bag, but by then, the cops had taken him for questioning. Since he was tied up for hours, I believe he used his phone call to tell Genevieve where we were. He probably hoped she'd save him the trouble and just fly into a jealous rage and kill us."

She took a moment to process all of that. "So, Collena isn't guilty of any wrongdoing?"

"No, I don't think so. Donnie wanted to make it look like she was a dirty cop to help his case."

Mia drew in a long breath. "He tried to ruin so many lives."

"But he didn't succeed." Logan leaned in and kissed her. Not a peck on the cheek, a full-blown kiss that eased some of her tension. "Once the police make sure it's safe to get us out of here, I'll take Tanner and you home."

"Home?" she repeated.

He lifted his shoulder and suddenly looked a little uncomfortable. That made Mia uncomfortable.

Oh, mercy.

She'd known from the moment she made love with Logan that they were going to have to face this. Where did they go from here? Yes, they had a child, but now that the danger had passed, they didn't have a real reason to be with each other 24-7.

Well, no reason other than she wanted to be with him.

Mia waited a moment to see how she felt about that and was pleasantly surprised to realize that she did indeed want Logan in her life.

But did he?

She probably would have launched into a mental debate, but the sound of the bathroom door opening put that on hold.

Dorien came out holding Tanner. Logan and Mia both got up and despite Logan's injured leg, they hurried to them.

But nothing was wrong.

Tanner was wide awake and looked perfectly content.

"I thought you might want to hold him," Dorien offered.

Mia agreed. She took Tanner, nuzzled his cheek and then immediately passed him to Logan. That eased some of the weariness in Logan's eyes.

It eased her, as well.

"I'll go check on Jason and the police," Dorien volunteered.

Mia welcomed the time alone. It was indeed priceless watching father and son bond. It was hard to believe that just days earlier she'd thought Logan wasn't father material.

She'd obviously been wrong.

"I want him to have your name," Mia said. Though before she heard the words leave her mouth, she hadn't known she was going to say it then and there. "Tanner Crandall McGrath. That's the way it should be."

Logan nodded. Just nodded. And she saw him swallow hard. "Thank you."

He didn't add any more, especially what Mia wanted to hear, so she decided to risk it. If she put it all out there and he refused her, then she'd just learn to live with it.

"Where's home?" she asked.

Logan lifted an eyebrow. "What do you mean?"

"You said after the police gave us the all clear, we could go home. Where's home?"

With Tanner cradled in the crook of his left arm, Logan slid his arm around her waist and led her to the bed so they could sit. Apparently, this was going to be a long conversation.

Mia automatically braced herself for the worst.

But then, she looked again at the scene in front of her and refused to give in to negative thinking. They were alive and they had their precious baby. It wasn't necessary to put labels and definitions on their relationship.

Even if that's what she suddenly wanted.

"Home can be anywhere you decide it is," Logan finally said.

She huffed. Then smiled at the firestorm of emotions.

"I'm in love with you," she said.

There. It was all out there now. Tanner was no longer the six-hundred-pound gorilla in the room. Her feelings were now the big thing they had to deal with.

Unfortunately, Logan's way of dealing with it was to stare at her and not say a word.

"Did you hear me?" Mia asked.

"Clearly." The corner of his mouth lifted and he reached out and skimmed his finger along her cheek. As usual, just that brief soft touch was more than enough to make her ache for him. "When did that happen?"

"When I had sex with you." But then, she shook her head. "It wasn't just sex."

He made a soft sound of contemplation, which could have meant anything.

"Would you like to know when I fell in love with you?" he asked.

Mia truly wanted to know the answer to that, but the question simply took her breath away. "You're in love with me?" she clarified, though she had to speak around the rather large lump in her throat.

"Very much so." He leaned in and kissed her. "I fell in love with you when I saw you nursing Tanner."

She thought back to that particular event and realized it'd happened before Logan and she had made love. "Really?"

"Really," he verified.

His voice was smoky and thick and his eyes fixed on her. With that heat and intensity simmering between them, Logan kissed her again. And again. The kisses probably would have continued if Tanner hadn't kicked at her arm. That little movement garnered both of their attention.

They looked down at their son.

"I want to get married," Logan said.

Mia's breath was already thin from the kisses and that statement made her even more light-headed. "Is that a proposal?"

"It is."

"Then my answer is yes."

The corner of Logan's mouth didn't just lift, it turned into a full-fledged smile. Mia realized she was smiling, too.

"Let's get married tomorrow. Tonight," he corrected. "We can fly to Vegas. Tanner can be our best man. And we can honeymoon in Fiji and then go home."

Oh, that did it. Mia didn't just melt, she turned to mush. "Sounds good to me."

"Which part?"

"All of it. Yes, to marriage. Fiji. And home." Mia had to blink back the tears. "So where's home?"

Logan slipped his hand around the back of her neck, eased her to him and kissed her until she was breathless. "Home is anywhere you are."

* * * * *

Next month, look for Delores Fossen's
THE HORSEMAN'S SON,
another book in her popular
FIVE-ALARM BABIES *series,*
only in Harlequin Intrigue!

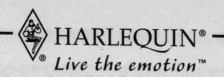

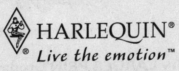

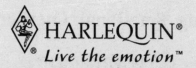

...there's more to the story!

Superromance.
A *big* satisfying read about unforgettable characters. Each month we offer *six* very different stories that range from family drama to adventure and mystery, from highly emotional stories to romantic comedies—and much more! Stories about people you'll believe in and care about. Stories too compelling to put down....

Our authors are among today's *best* romance writers. You'll find familiar names and talented newcomers. Many of them are award winners— and you'll see why!

If you want the biggest and best in romance fiction, you'll get it from Superromance!

Exciting, Emotional, Unexpected...

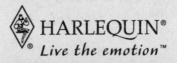

HSDIR06

HARLEQUIN®
Presents

The world's bestselling romance series...
The series that brings you your favorite authors,
month after month:

Helen Bianchin...Emma Darcy
Lynne Graham...Penny Jordan
Miranda Lee...Sandra Marton
Anne Mather...Carole Mortimer
Susan Napier...Michelle Reid

and many more uniquely talented authors!

Wealthy, powerful, gorgeous men...
Women who have feelings just like your own...
The stories you love, set in exotic, glamorous locations...

HARLEQUIN®
Presents

Seduction and Passion Guaranteed!

HPDIR104

 Harlequin® Historical
Historical Romantic Adventure!

Imagine a time of chivalrous knights and unconventional ladies, roguish rakes and impetuous heiresses, rugged cowboys and spirited frontierswomen— these rich and vivid tales will capture your imagination!

Harlequin Historical . . . they're too good to miss!

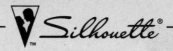

SPECIAL EDITION™

Emotional, compelling stories that capture the intensity of living, loving and creating a family in today's world.

Modern, passionate reads that are powerful and provocative.

nocturne

Dramatic and sensual tales of paranormal romance.

Romances that are sparked by danger and fueled by passion.

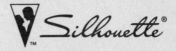